A LEAP INTO LOVE

"You'll do fine," encouraged the earl. "I'll help you."

"Unless you mean to jump it for me, I don't see how you can help me," Sophy answered him quizzically.

Without speaking another word, the earl turned and easily leaped across the stream which was beginning to look wider and wider to Sophia. He turned, stepped down into its muddy rooty lower bank and reached for her. "Come along then, I'm here to catch you."

She braced herself and with a little yelp made the jump. She reached the bank's edge on the other side and was about to laugh with pleasure when she felt the heels of her shoes slipping backward into the mud. "Oh!"

Just as she thought she was going for a swim, she felt the earl's arm gently encompass her and soon he was scooping her up to safety. They stood together for a moment before Sophy giggled and remarked, "I thought for certain I was about to become very wet." She made no effort to leave the comfort of his enveloping embrace and instead made a strategic mistake; she looked up into his glittering blue eyes . . .

A Rake's Folly

Claudette Williams

ZEBRA BOOKS
KENSINGTON PUBLISHING CORP.

ZEBRA BOOKS are published by

Kensington Publishing Corp.
850 Third Avenue
New York, NY 10022

First Printing: July, 1995

Printed in the United States of America

One

Miss Sophia Egan turned heads when she walked into a room. How could she not? Nature had blessed her with hair that was a beautiful and luxurious mantle of fiery red, and which she chose to style in a most charming array of wild disorder. Her face was a piquant picture of classic perfection. Her eyes were large, green and framed in thick dark lashes. Miss Sophy's height was, though not overly commanding, certainly tall. Her figure was a provocative line of curves that made nearly any gown she wore. However, a discerning eye noted that it was her smile that was her finest attribute. It would twinkle in her eyes, for it came from the heart, and won so many!

That was just what she was doing as she walked on her father's arm into Mrs. Bonner's ballroom. This was a particularly festive ball, as Mrs. Bonner was the mother of eight children, ranging in ages of seventeen to thirty. They were a well-liked, lively crew and Sophy was on close terms with any number of them.

Upon her entrance, the oldest, John Bonner, bent toward his brother to say softly, "Now . . . there is a woman! What a beauty . . . eh, lad?"

His brother sighed. "Yes . . . a fine lass, *fine.*"

One of Sophy's most ardent admirers, a local youth touched his best friend's shoulder and announced, "I am finished. Do you hear me, Oscar? If I can not have The Sophy, I shall die . . ."

His friend was not a romantic by nature and regarded him dubiously.

"Harry . . . you know, I don't believe it. Silly fellows, the pack of you, always ranting on and on about dying for love, but, damn if I ever knew a soul that ever has—"

"Nodcock! Did not Leander swim the Hellespont for Hero . . . because of love?"

"Did he?" Oscar shook his head of light brown locks. "Greek fellow wasn't he? Strange set, the lot of them and legends, you know, can't be trusted. Swam the Hellespont, indeed! I tell you what, if the poor fellow swam the Hellespont for this Hero woman, he'd be too blasted tired to do much more afterward . . . don't you think?"

Harry regarded him with great contempt. "Oscar, you are too cold-blooded to understand these things."

"Maybe so," said Oscar as he placed himself neatly in front of Sophy, bending low and coming up with her gloved fingers gently in his own. Two steps behind him his best friend seethed.

"Sophy girl, you are, as ever, completely ravishing," said Oscar. At his back, Harry considered kicking Oscar's derriere with some force. Only the knowledge that this would make fools of them both kept him in check.

"Oscar, how very sweet you are," said Sophy smiling first at him and then past him at Harry. They had been on easy terms for any number of years and she was never quite sure just how she should treat this new gallantry Oscar and Harry were recently exhibiting.

"Blister it, Oscar!" spluttered Harry, *"I* was going to tell her that!"

"Were you? Never mind, tell her something else," said Oscar amiably.

Sophy laughed. "No . . . instead, Harry, dance with me before Lord Gravesly catches me. He does make me feel so uneasy with his intense attentions." This was very true, but, it was also true that she wished to nip Oscar and Harry's dispute in the bud.

"With the greatest of pleasure!" said Harry triumphantly as he swept past his best friend to lead Sophy onto the dance floor.

"Now what is this about Gravesly?" Harry inquired when the steps of the cotillion brought them together.

She sighed. "He will not see that his attentions are unwanted. I don't want anyone to hear us . . . so we must not speak of it now."

"Right" agreed Harry, glancing in spite of himself toward Lord Gravesly and noting that the blackguard was staring at Sophy.

As the cotillion came to a conclusion and Harry led Sophy off the floor, he noted out of the corner of his wary eye that his lordship was moving toward them. "Here . . . we better hurry," he cautioned Sophy as he whisked her off in Oscar's direction.

Oscar was chatting with Harry's older sister and, spying them, the young man, with Sophy in willing tow, made a beeline for them. Harry held his sister's arm and unceremoniously bade her listen to him.

"Letty . . . keep Gravesly at bay will you? Sophy here don't like him, and what must he do but run her to earth! Charm him, keep him, only buy us a moment, that's the best of good sisters."

Letty had been married and on the town for nearly three years. She looked past her brother's shoulder and raised

one very pretty eyebrow. She had no great liking for
Gravesly. However, she was fond of her brother and liked
Sophy very well. She smiled teasingly. "La, Sophia, how
can this be? Why, Lord Gravesly is only thirty years older
than you," she pouted mockingly, "and has but one small
wart, or are there two on his nose?"

"Letty, you wretch." Sophy shook her head on a giggle.
"It isn't just that. There is something odious in his eyes.
I suppose I am being fanciful, but, he makes me so un-
comfortable."

Oscar had considered Letty's remark quite seriously and
interjected at this point, "Two . . . fairly certain, there are
two warts on his nose."

His friends eyed him disbelievingly for a moment before laughing. Letty stilled their mirth suddenly as she
raised her hand to whisper, "Go on then, for I see he is
nearly upon us." She was already stepping adroitly forward with her hand outstretched.

They heard her at their backs as they made their retreat,
"La, my dear Lord Gravesly. It has been an age, has it
not?"

They did not hear his reply as the three young people
slipped into an ante-room, one wall made up of long, lead-
paned glass doors leading to the garden.

Sophy laughed and her hands went to her hips. "Well, the
night air is lovely, but it is chilly and we certainly can not
stay out here all night." She peeped back inside the ballroom
and added, "Besides, I have it on excellent authority that the
Cortland Nabob is attending tonight. I must confess I have
been most curious to have a look at him."

"Ay . . ." agreed Oscar. "They say he is spending a
fortune restoring Cortland Abbey. Workmen coming and
going all week."

"And yet, very few people know anything about him," sighed Sophy.

"What do you want to know?" asked Harry superiorly.

"Harry? Never say you are acquainted with the nabob?" Sophy's green eyes opened wide.

"Well, no," Harry admitted reluctantly. "But, I know a thing or two about him all the same."

Sophia clapped her hands in some excitement. "Is it true that he actually fought a duel over a woman and was forced to leave the country?"

"Yes, that is very true," said Harry portentously. "However, there is more to the story."

"More? What more could there be?" Sophy asked incredulously.

"It was no duel in the *ordinary* sense, Sophy."

"Ordinary, Harry? What is ever ordinary about a duel?" bantered Sophy.

Harry's voice rose with excitement, "Only wait, Sophy, and I shall tell you." He shook his head, "I was scarcely able to credit it myself . . ."

"What?" demanded Sophy pulling her ivory silk shawl tightly round herself.

"The duel he fought was with his very own brother! Sophy, his older brother who was then the Earl of Cortland. The nabob was next in line to inherit the title and the estates. Zounds! You may well imagine everyone's shock." Harry shrugged, "Bad ton."

"Whew!" ejaculated Oscar. "Sticky business, indeed, but, I say, Harry, the late earl must have come out of the duel unscathed as that duel was over ten years ago. The Earl only died earlier this year."

"Don't know what injury he sustained in the duel. The family kept it all hushed up."

"Yes, I suppose they would," Sophy said absently as a frown pulled on her dark eyebrows.

"Hmm," agreed Oscar, "scandal and all."

"But there must be more to it," Sophy returned thoughtfully.

"The ironic thing is," mentioned Oscar, "here is Young Cortland, rich as a nabob and having to buy back the mortgage his late brother took on the estates."

"Aye," added Harry. "Young Cortland went off to India while his brother lived on to ruin their lands with poor management and wanton gambling."

"Yes, it is a pity what has happened to Cortland Abbey. Its gardens have turned to weeds," Sophy sighed.

"Well, not for long. They say the new earl is richer than the Bank of England," said Oscar. Then he added speculatively, "Wonder if that will sugar-coat his reputation and make him the County Marriage Prize of the season?"

"Oscar, how very awful." Sophia reproached him with word and look.

"Awful? Perhaps, but, probably true all the same," Oscar answered, staunch to his opinion.

"Don't know about that," stuck in Harry. "Has quite a black reputation to overcome."

"No doubt, but our society allows a *rich* man great license," Oscar returned knowingly. "At any rate, it will be interesting to watch and see."

"Well, we can not see anything at all from out here. I think we must return to the ballroom," laughed Sophy.

"Yes, but, what of the blackguard Gravesly?" Harry returned.

Sophy laughed again. "Oh Harry, I trust in you and Oscar to keep him at bay.

Two

Lady Amelia sat back against the rich dark brown squabs of the Cortland barouche and eyed The Cortland Nabob ruefully.

"La, Chase, you look as though you were about to be hung in the public square. Really, darling, it won't be so very bad."

He in turn eyed his pretty companion dubiously. "Won't it just!"

Lady Amelia laughed out loud and reached over to pat his white gloved hand. "Chase, you must show yourself socially, if ever you mean to still all the rumors and get on with your life here in England. Don't you see that?" She shrugged. "At any rate, this particular ball has always been rather good fun. The Bonners are a lively set and I am certain you will find an old friend or two amongst the company."

He eyed his cousin thoughtfully. She was his own age, two and thirty, yet she appeared so much younger than that. Marriage to his closest friend, Lord Arthur Burney, had done away with her shyness and given her a very attractive air of self-assurance. She and Arthur had remained his staunch allies through the years when most of his family and so-called friends had literally shunned him.

"As much as I adore you, Amelia, I dread walking into

that ballroom with you tonight," he answered and looked away, staring at his own reflection in the dark window of the coach.

"Well, that is not very flattering," Amelia teased. "I, on the other hand have been looking forward to making an entrance with you. Why, I shall be the envy of every eligible woman there. La, don't you realize that you are one of the two best-looking men in all of England?" She sighed happily. "How envious they shall be when you lead me onto the dance floor for the waltz!"

He laughed and flicked her nose. "One of two, eh? This other handsome fellow, who might *he* be?"

"Why, my dearest own Arthur," proudly smiled the lady as she found her coach door opened for her and a lackey waiting to help her gently out of the barouche.

Some moments later, having greeted the Bonners, they entered the spacious and brilliantly lit ballroom to the sight of undisguised interest, bold stares, shy glances, and open curiosity. Lady Amelia squeezed the strong arm she was holding. "Ah, I daresay our sense of fashion quite takes their breath away," she teased brightly. She then spied a good friend and smiled a greeting. It was Lady Jersey, who had been sojourning in Nottingham with her hunting cronies. As it happened Lady Jersey was very willing to meet and appraise the new Earl of Cortland. After all, she had heard about his great wealth and now she could quite see for herself that he was the very broth of a man!

Sophy had returned in time to witness the nabob's entrance. She stood back and watched his flitting expressions. She bent her head toward Harry and whispered, "Who is that pretty woman on his arm?"

"She is Lady Amelia Burney. No doubt his latest flirt," answered Harry pugnaciously.

"Well, only now look," put in Oscar with some surprise. "Old Silence herself!" Lady Jersey had already managed to strike up what appeared to be an enjoyable conversation with the nabob, and was in fact, turning round to call several others to her side to make his acquaintance. Lady Jersey was reckoned the Beau Monde's reigning hostess.

"Well, if she thinks *town* morals will do for us here in the country, she is in the wrong of it," said Harry in some disgust. "It will take more than Lady Jersey to win him a place in Nottingham."

"He already has a place, Harry," said Sophy softly. "He *is* the Earl of Cortland, remember?"

"Well, so he is," returned the young man irritably. "But that don't mean we must accept him."

"Harry, I did not think you so mean-spirited. We should not judge a man on cold rumor." Sophy frowned at Harry, but was immediately diverted by the sound of her name. She turned and scarcely stifled a sigh to find Lord Gravesly making a showy bow. Good manners urged her to allow him her gloved hand in greeting. Resigned, she had no choice but to give him the ends of her fingers.

"Enchanted, my dear," said Gravesly as his watery brown eyes scanned her figure. "Your ivory gown is a superb ornament for your flaming beauty."

Oscar leaned near to Harry and softly whispered, "See, *two* warts on his nose."

Harry nearly guffawed out loud, but both stood helplessly by as Gravesly insisted he lead Sophy in the next waltz, though Harry made a brave attempt to thwart Gravesly by interjecting, "Sorry, sir, this waltz is promised to me."

Gravesly regarded him with one grey brow raised high. "Ah, but, you will not mind giving over to someone who could be an uncle."

Oscar turned just enough so that only Harry could see him and rolled his eyes as he softly whispered, "Done up, on that."

"Uncle is it?" hissed Harry as Gravesly took over and moved Sophy off. "More like great-grandfather, I think!"

Sophy cast them a backward glance as Gravesly took her arm, but there was little she could do at that moment to save herself the discomfort of Gravesly's touch.

All this while Cortland had been watching Sophy's little group even as three young people had tried not to stare at him. This was in part because he had noticed Sophia nearly as soon as he had walked into the ballroom. He could see that these young people were probably no more than twenty years old, yet, were swayed to think poorly of him by rumors of something that happened almost twelve years ago. It certainly galled. Still, out of the corner of his deep blue eyes he watched the threesome and caught their exchanged glances, noting that the lovely redhead seemed distressed at the older man's obviously unwanted advances. He saw the manner in which Gravesly clutched the pretty girl's trim waist and understood at once.

Immediately he made an impulsive, but, sure decision as he excused himself from the gentlemen that had gathered round Amelia and Lady Jersey. With deft skill and great ease he managed the throng of people moving about on the dance floor. He tapped lightly on Gravesly's shoulder, but that gentleman turned and, thinking that the interruption was coming from Harry or Oscar, retorted harshly, "Take yourself off, halfling! I'll not be giving up my prize to such as you."

Gravesly was surprised to find towering above him a mountainous corinthian in a black coat that displayed to advantage his athletic form. Blue eyes glittered challengingly. "You may find I am *no* halfling—" stated the earl, who was then interrupted by the lady in question.

"And *I*, Lord Gravesly, am not *your* prize." Sophy pulled free of Gravesly's hold and allowed Cortland to deftly lead her off.

Sophy's green eyes were twinkling delightfully as she looked up at Cortland. "You can not know how very much I have been wanting someone, almost anyone, to rescue me from that man!" She was smiling warmly and thinking that he was even more handsome at close range.

His blue eyes shone as he noted her open appraisal, and he returned one of his own.

"Er . . . almost anyone? Even *the Black Sheep* of Cortland?"

She laughed brightly. He had a sense of humor; she liked that. "Are you telling me you are indeed the Black Sheep of your family, my lord?"

He grinned and inclined his head, "I am afraid yes, that is what my family calls me . . . when they are being kind."

"That doesn't make it gospel. At any rate, I must admit you are not at all what I expected."

"And dare I ask what you expected?" He was amused at her openness, and the frankness in her wide green eyes.

"Well, for one thing, I thought you would be older . . . *darker*."

"Darker?" He laughed, and then as sure dawning brought his thick ginger brows together, "Ah, of course, evil is associated with dark Satanic looks." A bitterness permeated the sad lining of his words, and the laugh vanished from his eyes.

"No, you mistake my meaning, my lord," Sophy answered honestly. "As it happens, I was not at all acquainted with your late brother, but I often saw him about. He was certainly very dark in complexion, his hair seemed very black, and his eyes were dark as well. You, however, are fair and have very blue eyes. Then too, you are much younger than he was, I think." She inclined her head. "And that is why you are not what I expected."

The smile returned to his eyes, and a chuckle tickled his lips as he found himself swirling Sophy lightly in the steps of the waltz. All at once he felt light-hearted. "Ah, so I am chastised. Indeed, my brother and I had different mothers. My father's first wife was of Spanish descent and Roland was much in her image. There were fifteen years between my half-brother and me." He regarded her ruefully, "Now, it is your turn, my girl."

"My turn?"

"Precisely so. You have me at a disadvantage. You now know a great deal about me and *I* don't even know your name."

She beamed, and then saucily dipped a shoulder as she answered him. "Quite right. I am Sophy Egan and much in your debt for I rather think you knew you were coming to my rescue when you cut in on Lord Gravesly."

He inclined his handsome head. "Happy to be of service . . . and so very pleased to make your lovely acquaintance." He smiled sadly. "However, as I am quite certain there are people who will warn you off such as I, our acquaintanceship may be short lived."

"Do you think so?" Sophy shrugged. "You may find when you get to know me that I have a mind of my own. I pick my friends . . . all of them."

The waltz had come to an end and Sophy found herself

suddenly surrounded by Harry, Oscar, and two of her very dear female friends. She turned to introduce Cortland to them, but he was already gone.

Her friends were squeaking questions about the nabob. Sophy's reply was to laugh and wave the questions off, but Harry made a fist and hissed dramatically, "Damn the impudent fellow's daring!"

"Who, Gravesly?" returned Sophy sweetly, knowing full well Harry was referring to Cortland.

"I think," said one of Sophy's pretty friends interrupting before Harry could respond, "that the earl is breathtakingly handsome."

"What?" demanded Harry spinning round in shock.

"Well, you can't argue that," said Oscar ever reasonable, "can you Harry?"

"I deuced well can!" snapped back Harry, much incensed.

"Well, I suppose you can, but it is a gapeseed thing to do," returned Oscar amiably.

The girls burst into giggles and Sophy announced brightly that people were going into supper. "Come along. I am famished!"

Three

Egan Grange stood in the shade of a green park, land-scaped gardens, and thick woods. The Georgian styled house was set on a peak and gracefully overlooked a narrow inlet of the Trent. Its furthest western boundary was marked by Sherwood Forest, and it was in that very direction that Sophia urged her spirited chestnut mare, for it was one of her wayward brother's favorite haunts. Ned had missed breakfast, and their father was anxious, for the morning had progressed into afternoon.

Egan Grange was not the only estate that touched Sherwood Forest. Cortland Abbey boasted a wide corner bordering the legendary woods. The renovations on the Abbey were coming along and the earl needed an escape from the trap he had created for himself. He made short work of it and saddled his black gelding himself. Moments later he was running his wild big black through Cortland's grassy fields to find himself, as he so often had when he had been a restless youth, at Sherwood. The Cortland Nabob smiled to himself and slowly guided his gelding through the woods to an opening in the thicket.

It was a glorious spring day. Daffodils bloomed in the forest beneath the sun's bright rays. He stopped his horse to enjoy the scent and sound of spring in the bud when a woman's voice caught his attention. There was something nervous in her tone, something strangely familiar in the sound. He quieted his fidgeting black and waited.

Sophy had only skirted the woods closest to the Grange. Ned had taken his pony and could be anywhere, but she rather thought he might be on his way home by now and did not wish to miss him. "Ned?" she called, and stood in her stirrups, for she was riding astride. "Ned?"

Sophy was dressed casually in an old dark blue riding ensemble. She wore no hat upon her flaming long curls, which were loosely tied to one side of her long lovely neck. The sun's bright rays enveloped her and the picture caught the earl's full attention.

"I don't answer to the name of Ned, but perhaps I may help?" offered the earl, and his blue eyes twinkled devilishly.

Sophy jumped and then the full impact of the earl's banter brought a flush to her pretty cheeks. Here was the Cortland Nabob. He had been a perfect gentleman when he had danced with her the night before. He had in fact rescued her from odious Gravesly, but now she was alone in the woods with him. What was she to do?

The earl understood at once and the smile faded, "Contrary to popular opinion, I shan't eat you, my dear." He also wore no hat upon his handsome head, but he bade her farewell with a slight nod.

Sophy felt abashed at once and reached her gloved hand out in his direction, "No, my lord . . . wait, please." Then she smiled invitingly.

He was not proof against her smile and inclined his head. "Of course."

"I am looking for my brother. He is only eleven and has been gone all morning."

Cortland's grin was boyish and it lit his entire face.

"Now, as memory serves me, I think I recall that when *I* was eleven years old, I managed to vanish from morning until dark without the least bit of difficulty." He saw the concern still hovered about her pretty face as he added, "Though, I don't recall having a school holiday at this time of year?"

A frown fluttered about her green eyes and she waved this off. "No, Ned doesn't attend school. He has a tutor who is at this moment pacing the corridors." She smiled apologetically. "However, I must not keep you."

"I can think of nothing I would rather do than spend a little time combing Sherwood Forest with you." He put up a hand. "Nothing wicked intended, I promise you. Really, you may use me at your will, and I *could* prove useful." He grinned, "You see, I roamed a good part of these woods as a boy and know them as I do my own land. Besides, two can cover a great deal more ground than one."

"Oh, thank you," Sophy smiled gratefully. "I accept your kind offer. Shall I start with this section and you take the portion closest to Cortland?"

"Right then." He produced a shining copper hunting horn from his dark leather saddlebag. "I'll blow this if I find your Ned. You can follow its sound." He saw the question in her eyes and shrugged a shoulder, "A relic from my hunting days."

She smiled and started off. It was well into the afternoon and she was beginning to feel some alarm.

He watched her for a moment as she started off and then moved his horse in another direction. There was a tree, Robin Hood's legendary tree, that lured boys and men alike to climb its heights. It was in the heart of the woods. Perhaps the lad had suffered a mishap climbing its lofty heights? However, the earl hadn't gone far when he came across a handsome pony grazing negligently. He scanned the area quickly and saw a young boy sprawled face down in the weeds and dirt. He jumped off his horse and hurriedly tethered him to a nearby branch. A moment later he was bending over the lad's limp body and calling his name, "Ned? Ned?"

The boy stirred and groaned. The earl lifted him to his thigh and touched the boy's face. He had a shock of red hair, freckles and a countenance that much resembled his beautiful sister. He opened his eyes and moaned, "Bouncer balked. I went over without him."

The earl looked round and saw the fallen tree the lad had evidently attempted to jump and grinned, "It's high and angled and no doubt the bright light put your pony off."

"Yes," agreed young Ned who squinted, "I was . . . am late, looking for a short-cut. Didn't take the time to steady him to the jump." He sighed. "M'sister would pull a face at me and say 'haste makes waste, Neddy.' And the shame of it is she always seems to be in the right of it." He then surveyed his benefactor and managed a shaky smile. "I am sorry. I am Edward Egan of Egan Grange. I am in your debt, sir," said Ned remembering his manners.

"The Earl of Cortland at your service, sir," grinned Cortland, with an inclination of his head.

"Never say so?" young Egan attempted to sit up, moaned and put a hand to his bruised head. He rubbed it and came up with blood on his fingers. "Whew . . ." he said boyishly as he inspected the blood. "I had better not let them see this when I walk in."

The earl noted that a trickle of blood had made its way

over Ned's ear and neck. He regarded him quizzically, "That, my boy, is the least of your worries just now."

"Ha!" returned Ned irritably, "If you only knew the way they cosset and nag after me."

"Now, I find that hard to believe. Your sister does not seem to be the nagging sort."

Ned grinned. "Not Soph! She is first-rate. It's m'father, and nanny and even m'tutor, Mr. Grimms." He started up again, felt a wave of dizziness and looking a bit startled sank backward and lay flat on the ground. "Feel a bit odd . . ."

"Easy now. You've taken quite a blow to your head, my little man, and shall no doubt need a stitch or two." The earl thought it was time he attempted to find Ned's sister. "Stay as you are, and try not to talk for a moment. I shan't be long."

"Yes, but, Zounds! The Cortland Nabob himself? All the World is talking about you," said Ned, innocently interrupting him. "But, you aren't a bit like people said—"

"Never mind that now, halfling. We had better make some attempt to get you home." The earl got to his feet and winked as he moved off saying, "Now, if you can keep still, I promise I won't be but a moment." Hurriedly he went to his horse and pulled out the copper hunting horn from his worn saddlebag and began blasting out its message.

"Famous! Are you a huntsman?" called out Ned pushing himself up on his elbow.

"Down!" ordered the earl as he returned to the boy's side. "Lie down and be still." He waited for Ned to obey and smiled, "I used to be a whip a long time ago." He looked round and blasted out a few more long notes.

"With any good luck your sister should hear that. She has been looking for you."

"Running me to earth like a baby," grumbled Ned. "It isn't right."

"Ditching your tutor, so that he has nought to do but pace the halls, isn't exactly fair either," suggested the earl amiably.

Ned grinned. "Did Soph tell you he was doing that? Lord save me then, I shall never hear the end of it."

The earl blew on his hunting horn once more. A moment after, he heard the sound of a horse crashing through the brush, and both he and Ned watched from different perspectives as Sophia Egan nimbly dismounted and rushed toward them.

Four

"Ned! Oh, Neddy," cried Sophia as she knelt to bend over him and touch his forehead, "what has happened?" She turned to look at the earl.

"Soph, don't be fretting yourself to flinders. It's not as bad as it looks. I've only had a little fall." He turned to the earl, "Do tell her it is nothing, my lord."

"Apparently your brother was in a hurry to take his fence. He and his pony did not quite agree on how it should be done." The earl smiled kindly. "What we need to do now is get him home and have his bruise attended to. I don't want to alarm you, Miss Egan, but, I rather think he might need a few stitches."

"Faith! Stitches?" Sophy took off her glove and gave his head a quick examination, "Oh my, Neddy, you are bleeding. We must get you home." She turned to the earl. "Can he ride, do you think?" She was already tearing off a piece of her white eyelet petticoat and binding it around the open wound.

"Of course I can ride!" snapped Ned wondering, in fact, if he could.

"No, he can not ride," said the earl with a threatening glance in young Egan's direction. "I mean to take him up with me, if that meets with *your* approval?"

"Yes. Oh, how very kind you are." Sophia was genuinely grateful, for she did not see how she could have managed without the earl's help.

Ned eyed the earl's black gelding with admiration. "By Jove, my lord, that's a bang up mount you've got there!"

"Let us hope you will still think so after you have been on his back," teased the earl as he bent to scoop Ned into his strong arms. "Hold tight, lad, you aren't exactly a featherweight!" bantered the earl, successfully banishing the boy's momentary embarrassment.

The journey home to Egan Grange was no more than two miles, but it was slow going and took twenty minutes to complete. When they reached the Georgian double front doors, Sophy jumped down from her horse and came round to assist her brother as he slid off the earl's mount. "Ned, perhaps you shouldn't walk?"

"For pity's sake Soph, don't treat me like an invalid. I'm fine." He looked up at the earl who was dismounting at that moment, "Prime blood, your black. What do you call him?"

"Ebony," said the earl briefly for he was preoccupied watching Ned limp heavily on his right side as he went forward. "What's this, scamp? Have you suffered a leg injury?"

There was a sharp stillness that suddenly permeated the air as young Egan turned. His eyes flickered with repressed feeling, but he released a short sigh and answered amiably, "No, that's just m'club foot. Had it since I was born." He turned and started off once more, shrugging off his sister's supporting arm.

Sophy's green eyes betrayed a flash of pain as she watched her brother's shoulders slump, but she relieved the tenseness of the moment at once by brightly smiling and saying to the earl, "Now, you don't really think you can return the prodigal son and escape without meeting our father and enjoying some refreshment, do you?"

The earl grinned and fell in with her banter. "By Jove, yes. I must say I would think myself very ill-used indeed if I were not wined, dined and treated as the hero I must be for managing such a wild creature as Ned here has proven himself to be!"

Ned turned at this and snorted. "Wild creature, eh? Well, you haven't met Grimms and Nurse." The front doors opened at this juncture to display a diminutive elderly woman, mobcap askew on her closely cropped grey curls. She stood with her bony arms akimbo beneath her dark wool shawl and demanded, "Well, young Egan, what have you got to say for—" At this point she noticed that there was blood about his ear, his neck and across one cheek. She threw her arms out and cooed, "My boy . . . oh . . . my poor darlin' boy!"

Ned groaned. "Blister it, woman. It's nought but the veriest scratch," he returned gruffly in the hopes of warding her off.

"Oh, my little man," responded Nurse as she enveloped him in her arms. "Such a brave, brave lad. Come now, and we shall see to your hurts. There, there."

"Soph?" called Ned in some desperation as Nurse attempted to take him away. "Soph, don't leave me to her. Soph, pity for your brother?"

Sophia laughed and adjured him affectionately, "Go on Ned. You must have that wound cleaned so that Doctor Halloway can stitch it up when he gets here." She turned to the elderly butler standing by and softly requested that he send someone for the doctor.

Stendly had been at Egan Grange when Sophy and Ned's father had been in shortpants. He took the liberty of a favored retainer and said, "At once, Miss Sophia, but you look as though the fire in the library might do you some good. I shall have refreshment brought to you there, if you like?"

She smiled sweetly. "I do like. Thank you, Stendly."

The earl had been watching these proceedings with interest and some amusement. He inclined his head at Sophy and said, "It is left to you to lead the way."

She sallied ruefully. "We must look sadly pampered and spoiled to you."

"It looks to me, that you manage to deftly wield a very caring and loyal staff. It is a wonder in one so young. As for being spoiled? I have yet to witness it in either your hearty brother or yourself."

She laughed and wagged a finger. "Yet, eh? Well, we are very spoiled, and I am not so very young, after all . . ." They had reached the library door which she opened and entered with a smile as she pointed to the sideboard. "There is a decanter of what Papa says is France's best brandy on the sideboard, please help yourself."

The earl glanced round the cozy room. Its oak beams stretched across the ceiling and made wide stripes down three of the four softly yellowed colored walls. A huge lead-paned window framed in brown velvet hangings trimmed with gold, overlooked a splash of garden at the far wall. Oak beaming made excellent shelves for books and various pieces of pottery which lined either side of the great stone fireplace. The room was warm and welcoming.

"This," said the earl with a show of his hands, "is a wonderful library!"

Sophy beamed happily. "Yes, isn't it? And it's mine!"

She laughed. "What I mean by that, is it's my favorite room in the entire house. My father has his study where he is forever at his writing. Neddy loves to rummage about the attic, but this you see, this is my very own sanctuary." Sophy's green eyes glittered. "My father says my mother felt the same way about this room."

The earl poured his brandy and raised the glass to her. "This room suits you, Miss Egan." His blue eyes glittered as he very definitely looked her over.

Sophia's intuition about people often guided her. She decided to give as good as she got. She lowered her lashes and then brought her green eyes to his face as softly she responded, "Well, and thank you, my lord."

The earl felt as though she had looked through his soul. He needed to break the sudden spell of the moment and immediately moved away, toward a portrait of a young woman in a blue riding ensemble. She was very nearly Sophy's twin. He looked from the portrait to Sophy. "Your mother?"

Sophy nodded. "Yes. Papa says I am her exact image, but there was a softness about my mother, an ease of grace that I shall never have." Sophy shrugged thoughtfully. "I am far too rough and tumble. Mama liked to stitch; I like to ride to hounds. Mama had good sense, born of patience, which evades me." She sighed, "I still miss her so very terribly."

"I am sorry. I did not mean to distress you." He frowned.

"Nonsense. My mother died seven years ago. It was very sudden. She went to her bed feeling not quite the thing and was lost to us by the morning." Sophy moved restlessly as the memory echoed in her mind. "Well, never mind . . . it was such a very long, long time ago, and I have been told often enough that time is a healer. It is true, at least for poor Ned as he was only four, and youth must win out. I suppose it was natural for him to turn to me. It was hardest on Papa. I don't think he really ever recovered from the loss of my mother. It was as though a light just went out in him. He turned to his books." She pulled a face and with a flutter of her hand shrugged the sadness off. "Faith! How morbid I must sound, and how awful for you to have to listen to me go on in this vein! Ah, here is our tray," Sophy said going toward the rich brown velvet sofa and inviting him to join her there.

It occurred to the earl that very easy manners ruled at Egan Grange.

Sophia was quick to read this flickering thought on his face and reassured him. "Nurse is, I am certain, still too busy with Neddy, and has forgotten that when last she saw me there was an unknown man keeping me company." She giggled. "However, you may rest easy. By this time, Stendly has made my father aware of his parental duty. I expect he should be joining us any—" She looked up as the library door opened, and smiled a warm welcome. "Papa, come and meet our neighbor, the Earl of Cortland."

Miles Egan was a tall, thin fellow with a shock of white hair. His nature had always been reticent, and studious. His late wife managed to bring him out of himself and, now and then, his daughter did so as well. For her sake, he would enter the social world, giving her escort, as he had the previous evening, to various local events. He came forward now, his hand extended. "My lord, I am informed that I have you to thank for my wayward son's safe return."

"Yes, indeed, Papa," put in Sophy, "the earl was kind

enough to help me search Ned out, and in fact was the
one to find him and then take him up on his prime black.
We are very much in his debt."

The earl waved this off with his hand. "Please, Miss
Egan is too kind. Taking Ned up on my prime black, as
your lovely daughter puts it, was not something I am certain Ned would thank me for, as he was jostled about as
Ebony pranced all the way here."

Sophy laughed. "Neddy loved every minute and so you
know, my lord!"

Miles Egan smiled benignly. "Well, I heartily thank you
all the same." He paused and then surprised his daughter
with his next remark. "I must tell you, my lord, I didn't
think to find you rusticating here in Nottingham."

The earl raised a brow of inquiry. "Did you not? May
I ask you why, sir?"

"Indeed, indeed." Egan hastened to repair any misun-
derstanding. "I had the good fortune to hear your eloquent
speech in the House of Lords. Liked what you had to say
and the way you said it. You raised an interest with the
damned Tories, and they don't often have anything good
to say about a Whig. You seem to have a flair for serious
politics. I thought to see you make your mark in London."

The earl inclined his head. "I thank you, no. London
and its weary politics is a sorry job for an honest man,
and whatever the World has dubbed me, I like to think I
might yet be too honest at bottom for politics." Then suddenly, abruptly, he put down his glass of brandy on a side
table and moved to make a bow to Sophy. In doing so he
had given her father his back and managed a rakish smile
for her. "I have overstayed. Forgive me, I must go."

Sophy gave him her hand and smiled apologetically.

"Of course, we have kept you far too long. Thank you, again, my lord."

Softly, for her ears only, he daringly answered, "Would that you might keep me still, but duty calls, even in the face of other desires." His blue eyes twinkled and then he was turning and going toward her father to shake his hand and say politely that he would show himself out. Sophy watched him leave, blushing hotly all the while.

Five

Miles Egan regarded his daughter warily for a moment. She was giving him one of her looks. "Well, what then?" he demanded, feeling it was better to get it over with. All he wanted was to return to his study and his work.

"Papa, this can not continue! Ned is too old for all your petting and coddling. Faith, he has a club foot, he limps, he is not confined to a Bathchair; don't confine him to the limits of the Grange. He needs to go off to Harrow, as his friends have done. You must not keep him here where he must end in kicking up his heels!"

Her father frowned and he put up his hand. "We have had this discussion before, Sophia. You know my point of view on the subject. Mr. Grimms is an exceptional tutor—"

Sophy got to her feet interrupting him irritably, "Papa, this is wrong. You are not being fair to Ned. You think he could not handle a little teasing about his foot? He can and should."

"I won't have him subjected to ridicule. Boys can be very cruel, and he has suffered enough."

"Father," said Sophia at her most impatient. "You can not shield him from life. You must not. It is time to cut line." Her voice grew softer. "Please, Father."

"Enough, Sophia. Enough." Miles Egan was so reminded of his wife when Sophy entreated him in this way.

It was almost more than he could endure. He turned and went to the door, saying only that he would be locked in his study for the remainder of the day.

Sophia frowned and shook her head as she watched him leave. This was unacceptable, yet what could she do? She had been nagging at her father for weeks to relent in his decision to keep Ned home another year. He wouldn't budge. Well, she thought as she got to her feet, she would not give up!

There was more to all of this than met the eye. Today had been the second time this week Ned had skipped out on Mr. Grimms and taken off for Sherwood Forest. It was time she and Ned had a little talk.

Harry and Oscar sat very straight in their saddles as they watched the Earl of Cortland take a short-cut through Egan's west field toward his own land. *"That,"* said Harry with disbelief in his light eyes, "was Cortland!"

"By Jove, yes!" agreed Oscar with something close to a frown. "What the deuce do you think he was doing at Egan Grange?"

Harry regarded his friend with a grimace. "What the devil do you *think* he was doing there? Chasing after my Sophy! That is what!"

"Not your Sophy. I know you would like her to be, so would I. That is to say, would like her to be *my* Sophy, not yours, but as of now, she ain't."

His friend cut him off with a growl. "Stop blubbering at me. We had better race on up to the house now before it is too late." Harry was in a jealous dither to be off as he set his horse to wildly canter toward Egan stables.

"Don't see what the blasted rush is for, the Nabob has

already been and gone," shouted Oscar reasonably in his friend's wake.

Harry did not answer him for he was no longer acting on reason.

Ned looked up from his writing and grinned saucily at his sister.

"Mr. Grimms has given me enough work to keep me up till midnight." He saw the look on her face and sighed. "Hallo, Red, come to read me a lecture? Well then, do your worst!" He regarded her almost defiantly.

She pulled out another wooden chair and sat facing him. "Now, Neddy, would I do that when I know you have heard enough from Nurse and Grimms to bluedevil you for, oh, shall we say an hour or two?" she bantered playfully.

He reached out for her hand. "Best of the best, Soph. I knew you would understand, but I thought Papa might have sent you up here to talk to me—"

"No, Papa is content to keep things as they are. I want to talk, not lecture you, love. I don't think you need lecturing. You know what is right and what is wrong, what you owe yourself, what you owe the family." Sophy shook her head. "No, what I want to talk about is what you have been doing. You are up to something Edward Egan, so don't try to fob me off with a Banbury tale, it just won't fadge!" She eyed him gravely. "Truth is what I shall have from you, dearest, just truth."

Ned considered her for a long moment. He adored Sophia. It was just as she had told the earl. He had turned to her completely after his mother had died for his father had been too lost in his own grief to comfort his children.

He had always trusted her, and he did so now. "Soph, you will say I am chasing windmills, but I swear I am not."

"Windmills? No riddles please," Sophia prompted him for more.

"Yes, but I can't tell you what I don't know. All I'm certain of is that there is a mystery in Sherwood Forest and I am determined to ferret it out," he said on a portentous note.

"Mystery? Sherwood Forest?" She eyed him dubiously. "Methinks there is an active imagination at work here."

"No, no, Soph. There is something going on. I've known it for weeks now, but I just can't put it all together. Someone is living in Sherwood Forest. I know it. I've seen the signs before he had a chance to hide them. I'm right, I know I'm right."

"Someone is living in Sherwood? Well, I suppose it is some poor soul who sadly has no home. There is nothing so very mysterious about that," returned Sophy gently. She didn't want to destroy his fun, yet, he must see the simple facts.

He shook his head. "Sophy, I'm not a dunce. That's what I thought at first, but tis more than that. This person holds secret meetings. I know. I hid in a tree late one afternoon and saw men sneaking into the Forest from different directions."

Sophy frowned over this for a moment. "Well, Sherwood Forest has been a magnet for many different sorts for any number of years."

"But, Soph, this is different. I mean to find out what they are doing," said Ned with determination.

Sophy didn't know what this was all about, but she wanted Ned well out of it. "Ned, if you are right and these are secret meetings, you could be in danger. I don't like it."

"Yes, I shall have to be careful," Ned answered thoughtfully.

"Careful? What are you talking about, careful? For all we know these characters could be cut-throats and thieves!" snapped Sophy. "Careful just won't do it, my boy."

"Yes, but, Soph, I don't mean to be caught."

A knock sounded at the schoolroom door and Sophia turned to find Stendly with the information that Mr. Harold Ingrams and Mr. Oscar Bently awaited her in the library.

"Thank you, Stendly. Please tell them I shall be right there." She waited only for the trusted retainer to leave before turning to wag a finger. "Ned, no more spying. Try instead to apply yourself to your studies. I want you ready for Harrow."

"Papa will never consent," her brother responded gloomily.

"We shall see."

Ned watched her go. Did he want to go to Harrow? John, his best friend was there this year and wrote that he had met some very fine fellows and was doing very well. Ned was lonely, more than even Sophy knew, but he was touched with fear when he thought of facing a group of strangers. He looked down at the enlarged shoe which hid his deformed foot. Perhaps Papa was right. Perhaps Harrow would not want him?

Six

Hedley was a diminutive Irishman. Fifteen of his fifty years had been spent caring for the present earl of Cortland. He was fiercely loyal and overly protective. Because he knew himself to be more friend than servant to the earl, he took a string of liberties without a second thought. He had become Chase Cortland's groom and acted as his valet when Chase had been still in his teens. He had willingly accompanied young Cortland when he had been resolutely and unfeelingly banished to India. It had always galled him that his employer had been the one to bear the brunt of *that* affair! He was fully acquainted with his employer's many faceted life. After all he had been there through all his employer's trials after that fateful day, twelve years ago.

He was about to take a liberty with the earl's newly installed butler, Woodly, simply in the spirit of mischievousness, when that worthy opened the front door to admit an extremely fashionably outfitted beauty. Hedley was immediately stopped in his tracks, and he stood with his mouth agape and his mind in a frenzy as he realized who this woman really was!

He had not seen her for twelve years, but he knew her at once. Had Hedley not thought her the Devil's own spawn, he might have noted that she was even more beautiful now, at nine-and-twenty, than she had been at seventeen.

She presented herself as Lady Anne and required the butler to announce her to the earl. Hedley's round hazel eyes nearly popped in disbelief. He watched her still as she glanced at herself in the marble hallway's long and gilded wall mirror. She pulled at one long curl of white-gold. Her pale blue chip bonnet and her traveling ensemble of the same shade of blue velvet was frogged and tasseled in silver making quite an outstanding frame for her trim figure. She knew herself to be quite stunning and moved with confident grace as the butler returned to lead her to the study, where he advised her the earl would receive her.

Hedley pulled a face over this piece of news. Well, he would have something to say about this, make no mistake! Receive the brazen piece of fluff? Calling herself Lady Anne and strutting about like a peacock when all the young earl's past trouble lay at *her* door!

In the meantime, Sophy had received her visitors, who, though they thought their Goddess as beautiful as ever, could not help but notice the dishevelment of her appearance. It was, in fact, Oscar who put up his quizzing glass and remarked in some concern, "I say, Sophia, did you fly your fence without your horse?" The old tease was in his eyes, for as youths they had often raced the fields and jumped the line fences together.

She looked down at her clothing and released a short laugh. "No, sir, I did not, but I do look as though I have, don't I? Well, that is what I wish to speak to you about,"

she said, as she drew them with her to the brown velvet
couch.

"What do you mean? You want to talk about jumping . . . oh! You mean the steeplechase coming up, don't
you? Well, it ain't for females. It's against the rules for a
female to enter and that's that, Soph!" returned Harry em-
phatically. Even for his darling Sophia, he would not be
budged in his opinion.

Sophia's dark brow went up. "That isn't what I want
to talk about just now, though, there is no saying that I
shan't want to talk about it in the near future. Really, it is
the outside of enough that women should always be excluded from anything a man deems unfeminine." She
waved this off in some exasperation. "Never mind that
now. What I want to know is what is going on in Sherwood
Forest?"

"Sherwood Forest?" returned Oscar openly startled.
"What are you asking?"

"Why should we know what is going on in the forest?"
asked Harry, narrowing his eyes and hoping to draw Sophy's attention to himself, for Oscar could not be relied
upon to maintain his composure in a lie.

"Because if anyone knows what's afoot in Nottingham,
you two do," returned Sophy. "Now, I shall ask again.
What is going on in Sherwood Forest?"

The earl had taken for his study a small ante-room off
the library which was housed on the first floor of the west
tower. This he had immediately converted into a room in
which he could work while restoration of the Abbey progressed. The stone walls of the room displayed ancestral
artifacts dating as far back as his family's early Norman

days. The round room housed a circular staircase that wound itself to a high second story tower floor where he could go to survey some of Cortland's extensive park. A large stone fireplace dominated one wall, and recently he had had his father's gothic desk refinished and installed in the center of the quaint, round room. Two leather-bound winged chairs flanked the sides of the enormous dark wood desk. No other furnishing adorned the room, and though many women might have thought it stark, the present Earl of Cortland was immensely satisfied with the results.

Outside, the noisy clamor of hammers and wood-sawing could be heard at different parts of the Abbey as the army of carpenters worked to restore Cortland to its former glory. It was what he wanted for his father's sake and the grandfather he still recalled with great affection. His brother had not cherished such sentimentality.

The earl looked up as his butler knocked, entered and quietly announced Lady Anne Bartholomew. He saw at once that the twelve years that had passed had not harmed her in any but the most subtle manner. Gone was the coy child, and in its place was the calculating woman. It was there in her measured smile. Still, there was no gainsaying that she was certainly exquisite. The earl got to his feet and went forward to take both her hands. "Anne," he said softly.

She went directly into his arms and kissed his mouth with a practiced passion she did not find at all difficult to feign with Chase Cortland. *Now* he had the title and, from all she had been told, the wealth she would need to keep her in the style she so enjoyed. She had always been attracted to his wild good looks and his tall, large, hard body. She came away from the kiss and gurgled with pleasure. "Darling, you have returned to me. I have missed you and thought of you all through the years." She sighed with a show of overwhelming feeling. "I rushed to you here," and now she lowered her lashes to her peachy cheeks, "even though it is not at all the thing for a young widow to visit a bachelor alone." She waved this off, "But I don't give a fig for that. I simply had to come as soon as I discovered you had taken up residence at Cortland. I wanted to welcome you home." Her gloved fingers ran down the length of his strong arm and found his large hand.

"It has been an eternity," Lady Anne whispered as she gave his fingers a light squeeze. She could not help but realize at this point that the light she had always seen in his eyes when he had looked at her in the past was gone. Well, she had known this would not be easy.

Gently the earl withdrew from her touch. Quietly he said, "I returned to England, to Cortland because of my love for home and country." He moved to his desk and leaned back against it as he folded his great arms across his chest. "You see my father's old retainer had sent word to me about the estates and how my late brother had left them in a sorry state of disrepair. I knew that since I had the means, it was my duty, and my desire, to set them to rights." Then, before she could chatter a response in that artificial way of hers, he said, "Lady Anne *Bartholomew?* I don't recall a Bartholomew on your lists?"

She sighed. "He wasn't. I met him shortly after you left England. I was so confused, so very unhappy. Sir Jasper was most comforting."

"I rather thought my brother was comforting you then?" He had not left England for nearly two weeks after

his confrontation with his brother and he had seen her in
his brother's arms . . .

She pouted. "He wasn't *you.*"

"Of course, you were pining for me," the earl almost
sneered. "Yet, I was told by . . . friends that my brother
was there for you."

"He tried, but then I met Sir Jasper . . ." she started
and managed to put on a face of pretty confusion.

"Who also was not," he bowed mockingly, *"me."*

"No, no, I always wanted you." This rang true, because,
it had been. "But my mother said you were only a second
son with no expectations." She bit her lip, annoyed with
herself for betraying this to him. "I would have disobeyed
her, had you stayed."

The earl was no longer a boy to be taken-in by such
lies. He recalled the past and all its glitter which had been
destroyed by truths too bold to deny. "Ah, and Sir Jasper
outbidded my brother who had the greater title, but not
the means to support a beauty," he looked her over audaciously, "with your excellent tastes?"

"I don't remember you being so vulgar," said the lady
turning up her chin.

"No. Then I was sprinkled with stardust, as were you."
He shrugged that off. "However, that was then and now,
now, Lady Anne, we have a different game."

"How many times must I ask?" pursued Sophy. She
took Harry's hand. "Harry, please. I am not asking out of
idle curiosity."

"Well," said Harry on a long note. "It isn't what a gentleman should be discussing with a gently bred lady."

"Gammon!" snapped the gently bred lady. "I must tell

you that Ned has discovered some mystery and means to go poking about the forest until he solves the mystery. I am not comfortable with that, and you can well imagine why."

"Devil a bit," agreed Oscar with some feeling. "I shouldn't let the lad do that if I were you."

"Well, try then to see if you can stop him," retorted the lady with some feeling. "Today he skipped out early, leaving poor Grimms to pace the schoolroom, and in rushing home he took a bad fall from his pony. Short of sending him off to school with his friends, where he really should be and which my father still refuses to allow, I am at my wits end to contain him. He is lonely and bored."

Oscar put a comforting arm about Sophy's shoulder. Harry noted this with a frown and became increasingly irritated as Oscar made an attempt to assuage Sophy's agitation.

"Blister it!" cursed Harry as he took his friend's arm and shoved it roughly off of Sophy's shoulder. "Must keep the lad out of the woods for a time. Especially in the late afternoons, and evenings. No telling what goes on."

"Ah, so you *do* know something!" accused Sophy.

"Perhaps we do," said Harry. "Perhaps just hearsay. At any rate, won't repeat gossip, but I will make you a promise to find out the truth of what we *think* we know."

"And then you will tell me?" Sophy was tenacious.

"Yes, then, I suppose we shall tell you. In the meantime, keep the halfling away from the forest."

Some moments later, as they walked to their horses in the Egan stables, Oscar frowned at Harry and said, "Now we have made a mull of it. She won't be kept at arm's length long, not Sophy."

"Yes, but there was nothing for it. At least we bought some time," agreed Harry with a grimace.

"When we finally tell her, she'll be dragging us into the forest. See if she don't. It's her way, hot at hand. Always has been, always will be," said Oscar philosophically.

"Sophy ain't what I would call a very restful female," agreed Harry sadly.

"That is a fact," nodded Oscar. "But she is a beauty. Did you notice how her green eyes flashed when she was ringing a peal over our heads?"

"By Jupiter, yes," sighed Harry "Only one thing to do tonight."

With that aim in mind, morosely they took to horse and made their way toward the village where they meant to spend a convivial evening at one of their favorite taverns. There, the ale would flow and the tavern wenches were dear amiable pretties ready to beguile. To the Red Hart!

Seven

Sophia noted that her young brother was none the worse for wear as they breakfasted together in the small breakfast parlor. Their father, however, seemed as much preoccupied as ever. Sophy tried to draw him out and bring him into their light morning banter, but though he smiled at his children, he did not join in their playful conversation. Sophy and her brother exchanged amused glances, and Sophy eyed her father teasingly. "Starting a new book, Papa?"

"What? Eh . . . oh . . . ah, book, of course," he answered absently.

Ned and Sophy giggled and then Sophy put her napkin on the table. "Come on Ned. Before you go up to Grimms, let's go have a look at Princess. She must be ready to drop that foal any minute."

"Zounds, yes!" agreed Ned as he followed her out of the room and they left their father to peruse his issue of the *Nottingham Gazette.*

"Did you talk to Papa? I know Mr. Dinkle wants to buy the foal, but do you think I may have this one. After all, by the time it is old enough to school to bridle and saddle, I'll be thirteen or so, too big for my brat, Bouncer, who is lucky I don't give him to the hounds after yesterday's stunt!"

Sophy laughed. "Scamp! You must learn to take your mount to a jump, don't be forever rushing your fence. Yesterday's fault lay at *your* door." She ruffled his bountiful head of red hair. "Yes, I spoke to Papa and he said that as he has no interest in breeding and such, all decisions regarding the management of our stables and horses were mine until you come of age. So," She pulled her dark wool shawl round her shoulders as the light spring breeze swirled suddenly and gave her a chill. Her green eyes twinkled at him. "I have considered your request, and . . ."

"Sophy, please. I should like it above all other things," begged her brother.

Sophy laughed as she relented and decided to give him her answer.

"Well, I was going to wait until the foal was here, but I shall tell you now. Yes, Neddy, you may have this foal. After all, since I took one of her foals for my own already, it's only fair you do the same. This one goes to you." She was smiling as he flung his arms around her.

"Sophy, this is what I want above all other things, a colt out of our Princess. How handsome he will be."

"Ned," laughed Sophia. "It *could* be a filly. There is nothing wrong with that. My mare has Princess's temperament and Bold Tim's lines."

"Ay, but if it is a filly again," said Ned screwing up his mouth, "Then you may sell it to Mr. Dinkle."

"Why, you little gapeseed!" retorted his sister incensed.

He laughed and hurriedly hobbled out of her way as she reached to pull at his hair. "Only bamming you, sis, only bamming. Filly or colt, *I want it.*"

She beamed happily. At least this would keep him occupied for a time. Perhaps it would be enough to keep

him out of Sherwood? Much in accord with one another
and the fineness of the spring morning, they veered toward the Egan stables. All at once, their hearts began to
pound and they stopped to watch as a young groom came
bounding round the corner of the side paddock in answer
to Jeffries' call. Jeffries, the Egan's head groom, could be
heard shouting excitedly and incoherently from the large
barn's confines.

Sophy and Ned exchanged wide-eyed glances and hurriedly rushed toward the open double doors of the stable.
As they approached Princess's large stall, Jeffries looked
up from the brood mare lying on her side on the straw.
He grinned wide, "Well, Miss Sophy, this be it." He ran
his age-weathered hand over the mare's nose and patted
her neck comfortingly. "Coo now lovely. There now,
pretty, ye'll do, course ye will."

The Earl of Cortland was at that moment trotting his
black up the long winding front drive of Egan Grange.

The gatekeeper's wife noted to herself, and then out
loud to her worthy husband, that here was the very broth
of a man. Indeed, the earl was looking very well in the
buckskins he had chosen to don. His dark beaver top hat
sat rakishly on his silver-flecked fair tresses, and there
was no denying he rode his horse in fine form.

The earl veered off and took the short wide path to the
quaintly styled Georgian stables, thinking to walk up to
the house from there. However, when he reached the stable, no groom was to be found to take his horse. Nimbly
he dismounted and led his horse within the stable, calling
out as he entered through the open double doors, "Hallo?"

The young groom avidly watching the proceedings in

the foaling stall blushed and rushed toward the earl, apologizing as he took the reins from the earl's gloved hands. "Lor I'm that sorry m'lord. Didn't hear ye ride up. Would ye lyke yer blood stalled then wit some hay?"

"Thank you, yes. I'm just going up—"

"Over here, my lord," called Sophy recognizing his voice with a fluttering heart. Something was seriously wrong with Princess. The mare's labor was strained and, while she had gotten to her feet twice, she had come down again. It was beginning to look as though Princess would need help. Jeffries was more than a little concerned, as he told Sophy he was going in to help the foal along.

The earl looked round and moved toward the sound of Sophy's voice in the foaling stall. Vaguely it occurred to him that she had a warm, sweet tone, almost musical. He frowned at the notion. Never mind. She was just a child, no more than nineteen or twenty he was certain, and he, well, he was a seasoned rake of two-and-thirty. However, all such cogitations were banished as he surveyed the scene that next met his eyes. This mare was in trouble. He knew the signs. The mare was on her side, she was struggling in some distress. Ned was holding her long black tail up while Sophy worked at wrapping it. Without speaking the earl immediately bent to the mare's head and gently touched her nose. He could see the pain in her eyes. He looked to the aged head groom who was on his knees by the mare's belly in the straw. "How long has she been like this?"

"Thirty minutes or so, but I just went in and the sac is still holding."

"What was the foal's position?" The earl's voice was authoritative and yet set the old groom at ease.

"Well now, that's just it, wasn't sure, couldn't find 'is

nose. But, well, wasn't backward neither . . ." Jeffries scratched at his stubbled chin.

The earl was shrugging out of his coat, rolling up his shirt sleeves as Sophy stood out of the way and watched in some surprise. He was down on his knees a moment later and going into the mare.

After what seemed an eternity to the three watching him, Cortland spoke softly to the struggling mare as she was trying to get up.

"There, there Mama, your foal is fine, he just needs a little help."

Suddenly Jeffries shouted out in some agitation, "Now we're in the basket. 'Er water broke."

Indeed, there was a rush of water that surged round and soaked the straw at her back legs, but the earl moved quickly, shifting the foal's nose and front legs into position. This done he strained as he pulled.

"Grab a hold of me," he shouted at Jeffries, "and get ready to pull as I do."

All this while Sophy and Ned couldn't speak. They watched the earl and then looked at one another. Here surely was a man like no other they had ever known. Sophy could not help but notice his brilliance, his strength, his gentleness, his concern, his willingness to get down in the dirt and the blood. She found herself suddenly, for the first time in her life, very impressed.

Then suddenly the foal's forelegs and nose emerged and Ned and Sophy screeched with delight as they hugged one another. The earl and Jeffries fell back. The foal lay thoroughly exhausted in the straw, but everyone could see that it was a big, healthy, beautiful foal. The mare snorted feebly and bent her neck with effort as she looked round at her new babe. Ned gasped with delight as he fell to his knees and stroked the wet new wonder. He turned a joyful face to his sister and declared excitedly, "Its a colt, Soph, a colt!"

"So he is." Sophy laughed and turned to the earl to extend her hand. "Thank you seems infinitely inadequate. You arrived just at the right moment. What exactly was wrong?"

There was a smudge of dirt across Sophy's pretty white cheek, and her fresh morning gown of lime green was soiled as well, yet it flashed through the earl's mind that she was the most beautiful woman he had ever beheld. Automatically he set up a barrier between them; beauty was not something that would ever ensnare him again. "He was out of line, at right angles to the right direction. We just had to better position him in order to help him enter the world." He glanced at her shawl which was now quite ruined as it lay in the straw. "I am afraid your pretty shawl is spoiled. I trod it underfoot."

She laughed. "It is a small price to pay for a miracle, I think. It would appear that I am forever finding myself in your debt. Thank goodness you came along. You are always coming to the rescue." She shook her head. "Princess dropped foals twice before. Both times she did so when she was leisurely grazing in the fields and when we least expected it to happen. She had no trouble whatsoever."

"Mother Nature is a female." He grinned wickedly as he moved away and bent to take up his coat from the straw.

"Meaning?" Sophy's hands went to her very fine hips.

"Meaning that she is beautiful, but very mysterious. One should never try to outguess her." He winked. "It leads to trouble."

Sophy smiled and said, "All jesting aside, my lord, *you* outguessed her, didn't you? You knew what was wrong and you knew what to do." Sophy's green eyes were warm with admiration and no little wonder.

"My father was an avid horseman. When he was alive, we bred horses at Cortland. I learned a great deal at his side." He moved further from her still. "I am having the stables rebuilt and hope to start a breeding program eventually."

"Soph!" shouted Ned drawing everyone's attention. "Look, he is getting up already. What a brave fellow!"

The colt had staggered to all four legs, wobbled, fell spread-eagled and immediately repeated the entire process. Princess put her head up and with something of a groan got up and shook herself. After a moment she was nudging her foal and whinnying softly to him.

Sophy clapped her hands joyfully. "Oh, isn't that the most beautiful thing." She turned and took hold of the earl's hands to squeeze them. "Thank you. I can't think what could have happened had you not come by."

He frowned. "You make too much of it. It is I who should thank you and your brother for affording me yet another adventure. Here I was thinking to pay a simple call and instead was given an opportunity to er, play with Mother Nature."

Sophy found herself blushing with pleasure. He had come to call. Shyly she gave him the bait. "How obtuse of me. You must have come to visit my father, and here we are keeping you—"

He put up his hands, "Not at all. I came to call on Ned and see how he was doing after his escapade yesterday." He grimaced at young Egan. "However, I can see he is doing much better than even I expected. Up and about and the proud owner of a newborn colt, eh my friend?"

"Yes," said Ned happily as he stroked the foal. He eyed the earl. "Doesn't our Princess put out wonderful foals, my lord?"

"She certainly does, lad."

"If you mean to start up your breeding farm, my lord, you might want to use Princess as a brood mare," Ned offered brightly.

"Ned!" objected his sister, her cheeks going bright red.

"I certainly couldn't do better, and that is a fact," said the earl waving off Sophy's objection. He had to keep this one at a safe distance, he thought as he gazed at Sophy. Her wide-eyed innocence was far too appealing.

Sophy had been conscious of a moment's chagrin. She had thought perhaps, just perhaps, the earl had come to pay her a morning call. However, it had not been so. He had only come to see Ned. She was feeling oddly shy and embarrassed by such absurd notions. Never mind, she told herself. What would this sophisticated, incredibly handsome mountain of a man want with her? Still she managed to do the polite and invite him up to the house for refreshments.

He smiled apologetically. "I am afraid I can not. I'll just clean up and then I have some business in town that needs my immediate attention." He was shrugging into his coat.

Sophy had never felt insecure or inadequate. She did now for she did not quite believe him. There was a coolness in his manner, a retreat in his bright blue eyes. She turned away from him and thought she no doubt bored him. After all, she was just a country miss and he was a well traveled rake who had his pick of women. She put up a pretty brow at her brother. "Well, it is time you made your way to Mr. Grimms, Neddy, don't you think?" Placing an affectionate hand on his shoulder she said, "Come on I will walk up with you and explain why you are late."

She sent her shyness to perdition and turned to extend her hand to the earl. "Thank you, again, my lord. I only hope we have not made you late for your appointment." She returned his sudden aloofness with a measure of her own.

"No thanks needed, Miss Egan. It was my pleasure to be of service," he answered seeing a definite withdrawal in her demeanor. Well, there was nothing for it. He moved out of the foaling stall and requested the young groom to prepare his horse. His hands were still sticky with dried blood. Sophy had been heedless of the blood and the dirt when she had taken his hands. A most unusual female. He dipped them in a nearby bucket of fresh water, washed them clean and dried them on a discarded rag. That would have to do for now.

"Soph, I want to stay with my colt," Ned complained, as his sister led him out of the stall.

"Your colt needs to be with his mother. Look, she is washing his face." She sighed happily and ruffled her brother's red crop of hair. "'Tis time you went off to your lessons and worked on giving your foal a proper name."

"A name?" Ned looked puzzled. "A name." He then beamed happily. "I shall call him Intrepid, for he was a brave thing, wasn't he, Soph? Pulled and tugged into the world. Brave boy, yes, he shall be Intrepid." He bent to give the foal a parting rub that nearly capsized the unsteady creature. Brother and sister burst into mirth, and then with one last look at the foal, they started to exit the stables.

Ned stopped Sophy all at once and turned back to call, "My lord?"

"Yes, Ned?" the earl was leading his horse out of the stable, not far behind them.

"May I come up to Cortland soon and have a look at what you are doing with the stables?"

"Ned, you can't go inviting yourself up—"

"But of course he can. I should like that Ned," the earl interrupted her objection and then, without knowing how the words entered his brain and then emerged from his lips, he found himself asking Sophy, "Perhaps, Miss Egan, you might like to accompany your brother to Cortland. I would be happy to show you what we've already managed to accomplish at the Abbey."

"Perhaps, my lord," was all the answer Sophia was about to give him then.

He watched them walk away and called down a curse upon his own head. Common courtesy required that he invite her as well. It was no more than that. He was not going to bother his head about it. His invitation meant nought.

Eight

Just facing Nottingham Circle reposed a square stone building with lead-paned windows. It was a quaintly styled two-story building and was most charmingly covered in dark green ivy. Over its door a simple, but elegant, brass displayed the name of Harcot and Harcot, Solicitors at Law.

The passing earl heard his name called and looked up to salute an old acquaintance. He smiled to himself as he entered his solicitor's office. There was a time the old stickler would not have acknowledged him. Riches had such power. Sad, but, proven true over and over.

As he entered and stepped into the long hallway, a young clerk sitting within the confines of a small cluttered office got to his feet and promised to fetch Mr. Harcot at once. The earl again smiled to himself. The youthful clerk was evidently in awe of the reputation that preceded Cortland. A moment later he was met by the younger Harcot who advanced, hand extended as he smiled a greeting to their firm's most prestigious client. His father had been representing the earl's legal interests for any number of years. When Cortland arrived in London more than six weeks ago, old Mr. Harcot himself had been there to meet him. The elderly gentleman had been the earl's first caller some weeks ago upon his installation at the Abbey, however, this was young Harcot's first meeting with the man. He thought that his father had given a very accurate description, for there was no mistaking who this tall self-assured aristocrat could be, and Harcot found himself immediately impressed.

"My lord, welcome. I have been looking forward to this meeting. I am Thadeus Harcot. My father has not returned from London, yet, but, I trust that you may be satisfied with my services in the meantime?"

The earl regarded the younger man candidly. He looked to be a bright, capable and pleasant fellow. He smiled amiably and returned Harcot's warm grip. "I have no doubt of it."

Harcot led him to his office and gesturing to a large leather-bound winged chair, smiled as they sat and faced each other. "Well, my lord, how may I help you?"

Oscar and Harry rode their horses at a sedate pace as they made their way to Egan Grange. True to their word they were returning to answer Sophy's burning question about the goings on in Sherwood Forest. Harry regarded Oscar morosely. "Well then, we are agreed?"

"I suppose." Oscar tended to be laconic on subjects that he was loath to discuss.

"Yes, but do you think it will serve?" Harry's nature was quite the opposite. He would talk a thing to death.

"I suppose."

"Why? You know that Sophy plunges into things head first, always has. Remember that time when we were twelve and on our way to the sweet shop? There was that scene across the street. The animal was only a mongrel after all. And deuce take it, the villain was a brute of a fellow all dirt and grime. Did that deter Sophy? Do you remember?"

"One does not forget incidents like that," said Oscar ever reasonable, "I am sure I stopped breathing throughout the entire ordeal."

"By Jove, yes, but the thing is she dove right in, snatched the cur in all his filth to herself and wagged a finger at the scoundrel as though he were a child. He looked as though he might kill her when he raised his hand, but did Sophy even flinch?"

"Not she," said Oscar recalling the incident vividly and in some awe.

"Right. Bluffed her way through with some threat or other and the fellow took himself off. Not the point, though. The point is he could have struck her. She could have been hurt. If we tell her what is going on in Sherwood Forest, I'll wager a monkey, she'll dive right in. It's just the sort of thing to attract her."

"Well," agreed Oscar sadly, "that's the truth of it, right and tight."

Sophy had bathed and changed her soiled dress for a pretty day gown of pale blue. She made her way to the library and idly picked up a book, then greeted her father warmly when he stuck in his head at the open door to say he was going out.

"Oh, into town, Papa? Shall I go with you? I have been wanting to get into town and try on my new gown. It must be ready by now."

"Er . . . well, no. I am going over to the vicar's. He has some material that he prepared for me. Thinks I might be able to make some use of it."

Sophy sighed but threw her father a kiss and resigned herself to a quiet afternoon. Never mind, she told herself, she wanted to catch up on some reading. It was therefore with a great deal of enthusiasm that she greeted her friends when Stendly showed them in. "Harry, Oscar, Princess had her foal this morning and just wait till I tell you about it." She had bounded forward happily and took hold of each of their arms.

She was interrupted, however, by Oscar who requested with some intensity, "Filly or a colt?" He turned to give Harry a self-assured glare. *"Now,* we shall see."

"A colt, but—" answered Sophy frowning slightly but was cut off once more.

"Aha!" breathed Oscar triumphantly as he turned to his comrade.

"That is another coin you owe me, old boy."

Harry grimaced at him sourly. "Blast you."

"Yes, well you should have known better than to bet against me. Have a feeling for these things. This is the third foal I've called this season," Oscar said puffing up proudly.

"Are you two quite ready to hear what I have to tell you?" stuck in Sophia icily.

"So sorry, Sophy, forgive us?" returned Harry taking her dainty hand to his lips.

Somewhat mollified, Sophy's eyes opened wide once more as she recanted the morning's events and ended with, "Can you imagine? I don't think Intrepid, for that is what Ned calls him, would be alive if the earl had not come then and taken care of everything."

Justly, Oscar gravely gave it as his opinion that he thought this was so. Harry, on the other hand, jealously demanded, "What the deuce was that nabob doing, coming here?"

"Oh as to that, he came to call on Ned," said Sophy lightly.

"What the devil did he want to do that for?" Harry pursued.

"It is only natural," answered Sophy in some surprise. "After all, *he* was the one who rescued Neddy yesterday and brought him safely home."

"Only natural." Oscar was ever socially correct.

His lifelong friend stared him down before returning his loving gaze to Sophy's face. "Well, Soph, we have that information you wanted, about what might be going on in Sherwood Forest." There was a portentous sound to his words that caught her full attention.

"Sit, sit at once and tell me everything," Sophy demanded in some excitement.

Oscar and Harry exchanged wary glances, but there was nothing for it; they did as they were bid.

"These things can be done quickly, but as you wish to keep your name out of it, and I quite agree that might be wise, it may take a bit longer." Harcot was frowning as he stroked a letter opener thoughtfully.

The earl sat back in the winged chair and regarded his young solicitor. He liked the man very much. "Well then, how long do you think it will take you to uncover the information I require?"

"I should not think it would take more than two weeks, perhaps, three at the most."

The earl got to his feet. "Good, I want to get started

with this as soon as I may. I leave it in your capable hands, sir. Thank you."

Harcot showed him to the door and waved him off, but the earl did not immediately return to the livery for his horse. There was some shopping he needed to do first.

Lady Amelia spotted the earl crossing the avenue and called out as she walked toward him, "Chase?"

The earl turned to beam warmly, "Amelia . . . what a very fetching bonnet. Your taste is as always unimpeachable." His eyes lit up suddenly. "And you are just the woman I need! What are you doing? Can you spare me a few moments?"

"Well, yes, if you promise to join Arthur and me for dinner tomorrow night?" she blackmailed sweetly.

"Done!" grinned the earl taking her arm and pulling her along.

"Luddites? Here in Nottingham? I rather thought their movement was centered further north of us?" returned Sophy upon being told that members of the Luddite Movement were rumored to be holding secret meetings in Sherwood Forest. She was frowning darkly. From all she had read, these were a group of desperate people that had turned to organizing riots and violence. She didn't want Ned coming upon them in the woods.

"Can't really tell you much more," Harry returned with a shrug of his shoulders. "I'm not even sure it is true. Haven't witnessed anything first-hand, you see." As soon as the words were out, he knew he had made a mistake and began to squirm.

"Yes, but it doesn't make sense. Why should they meet here in our woods? Luddites are members of the working class, with some very genuine grievances. However, it would make more sense for them to meet in the cities, would it not?"

"Don't know about that," Harry returned warily trying to remain on safe ground.

"Yes, well, as to that, there is some sort of fellow they are calling King Ludd; meeting at Sherwood because of him." Oscar could see Harry glaring at him from the corner of his eye. That was all that was needed to attract Sophy's attention.

"King Ludd? Never say so? Why, how very exciting. Who is he?"

Harry shrugged. "No one knows. At least no one is saying."

"But why do they call him King Ludd? What does he do? Plan their riots and machine smashing?" Sophy was ever tenacious.

Oscar started to speak but was nudged by Harry who shrugged once more and quickly answered, "Who knows, Soph, it is out of our ken. No need to worry about Ned, no doubt they only meet in the dead of night."

"You think they meet at night?" Sophy's delicate dark brow was up as she thought this out and shook her head. "But how could they find their way in the woods when it is pitch black?"

Again, Harry could have bit his tongue. "Don't know. I'm probably off about that, you know."

Oscar put up his hand as though he were in school, but didn't wait to be called on as he quickly gave his opinion. "No doubt use lanterns."

"Of course," said Sophy touching his arm. "How clever you always are Oscar."

"Clever is he?" snorted Harry. "Clever isn't what I call it, diving headlong into business that don't concern us."

Sophy pooh-poohed this and said with determination, "Well, we must make it our business to discover their whereabouts. Plotting riots and other forms of violence is criminal and we must not allow that to happen in our beautiful Nottinghamshire."

Harry and Oscar eyed one another and then Harry put a hand on her shoulder. "Sophy, be reasonable, we can't go snooping about at night in Sherwood Forest."

"Why not?"

"Luddites wouldn't like it," said Oscar logically.

"Yes, but, we *must,*" returned Sophy undaunted.

"Don't see that," answered Oscar. "None of our affair."

"Oh, but Oscar, it is. It is our duty," cried an impassioned Sophy.

"There's the rub," said Oscar. "Duty."

Harry glared dangerously at Oscar and then raised his light blue eyes heavenward. This had not gone well.

Nine

Oscar and Harry had only just left Sophy when Stendly reappeared at the library door to announce, "Mr. Nathan Walker."

With a clap of her hands Sophy jumped to her feet and hurried to the library door to throw her arms about Mr. Walker's neck. "Nathan, you miserable wretch! You never answered my last letter and here you are!" She stood back to better survey him. "La, but you do look every bit the London beau, don't you?" She tweeked the lapel of his blue coat and laughed adorably. "A veritable fashion plate."

He smiled and took both her hands to his lips. "I did not write because I thought I would answer you in person, but if you are going to ill treat me, I think I shall quickly make my exit." He started to turn away.

She grabbed hold of his arm. "Don't you dare." She laughed and linked her arm through his. "Come, sit with me, Nathan. When did you arrive?"

He pulled a rueful grin and evaded the question, saying, "I would have been here sooner, but I have been working like mad at the Abbey and have had to do some posting about between Nottingham and Leicester, looking for all the various building materials we need."

"The Abbey?" Sophy's green eyes opened wide.

"Never say *you* are the architect in charge of the renovations at Cortland Abbey?"

Mr. Walker pulled himself to his full height, which was substantial, and made her a mock bow. "At your service." He then went on to say, "The earl came to me in London and told me my name had been highly recommended to him. He also felt I had an advantage over other, perhaps more experienced architects, because I am from Nottingham."

Sophy was tall but still had to get on her toes to kiss his cheek.

"Congratulations! Well, you have made quite a wonderful reputation for yourself in the short time you have been established on the town. I am ever so happy for you." There was a time when Sophy had been just a schoolgirl and she thought the sun rose and set with Nathan Walker. Now he was six and twenty, well built, pleasant looking, and very, very dear. She regarded him with a flirtatious light in her eyes, "So, how long have you been here before you condescended to come to Egan?"

He laughed. "Sophy, I won't tell you for you will wish to fry me if you knew. Believe me, I have been gone more than I have been here. If I wasn't staying with my father in Nottingham, I don't think I would even have seen *him* . . . the two or three times that I have."

She shifted her shoulders and pursed her lips. "I suppose then that I forgive you."

He threw back his head with laughter and took her shoulders in his firm grip. "Sophy, you devil."

It was late, perhaps too late to stop by Egan Grange, for it was nearly four in the afternoon. In spite of that, the earl set himself in the direction of Egan and knew a ridiculous sense of pleasure as he turned onto the drive. He trotted his horse to the stables where a young groom hurried over to take the reins from his horse as he dismounted. The earl smiled and flipped a coin to him as he untied his package from his saddle strap, and then he was briskly walking the distance to the house, happy to discharge his errand and be done.

Once there, he faced Stendly and asked where Miss Egan was. Upon being told that she was in the library, he merrily walked past the elderly retainer, saying that he knew the way. Stendly was quite used to Sophy's friends forever charging in and out of the house and saw nothing incongruous about this behavior. Thus, it was that the earl marched into the library to discover Sophy very nearly in the arms of his architect. The earl was surprised, then thoughtful as he watched the two spring away from one another.

"Forgive me. I intrude." He took a step backward.

"My lord," said Sophy on a note of amusement, "you certainly do not intrude, but I am surprised, pleasantly so, to receive you here twice in the same day." Her brow was arched quizzically. She had not thought to see him at Egan again for a long time after his cool aloofness of the morning.

The earl took her welcoming fingers and put them lightly to his lips; he was conscious of the scent of spring flowers. He looked up to smile at her and then for the first time at Nathan Walker.

She turned to Walker and saucily said, "I believe no introductions are necessary?"

"Devil," muttered Walker as he stepped forward to shake the earl's extended hand. "Miss Egan," he turned to grimace at her, "and I are old friends, and this is the first chance I have had to call on her." A sheepish smile curved his lips. "In truth I left the Abbey early in an effort to escape you before you returned. I dreaded what you might say when you saw how little was accomplished today."

"Ah, Nathan, the moldings did not arrive?" the earl shook his head. "So be it, they will."

"You are most understanding. I suppose I have the presence of a lady to thank for that?"

"Never say the earl cracks a harsh whip?" returned Sophy half teasing, half in earnest. "I would not have thought it."

Walker relented at once. "No, indeed, Sophy, at least I have not seen him do so. In all fairness, he certainly has had reason to be disappointed with some of our progress. We have had the devil's own work trying to get in all the supplies that we need."

"Nonsense." The earl inclined his head. "Nathan is far too modest. He constantly surprises me with all he has been able to accomplish in these past weeks. Everything has been coming along very smoothly, thanks to him." He shook his head. "I think the man is fishing for a compliment because of the presence of *this* lady."

Walker laughed and took a step toward Sophy. "And on that note I mean to make my exit. It is good, so good to see you, Soph." He was bending over her fingers.

"But you will come by again?"

"How could I not?" He hesitated and looked toward the earl. "In the meantime, perhaps, my lord, Miss Egan could ride up to the Abbey for a visit and I could show her all the renovations you have instituted at Cortland?"

"Indeed, I have already extended an invitation to both

Miss Egan and her brother to visit us at the Abbey." The earl was surprised at the gruffness he heard in his own voice. What the deuce was wrong with him?

Walker bowed himself off and was gone a moment later. The earl felt himself frowning and made an immediate attempt to banish his illogical irritation. There was no cause for it. It was absurd. He liked the young architect, indeed, he had even felt he and Walker had been developing a friendship. Certainly, Walker was not only an excellent architect, but a damn pleasant fellow as well. Yet, there was no denying the relief and pleasure he felt when he watched the younger man take his leave. No doubt, it was only that he wanted to discharge his errand and be gone himself?

In this frame of mind he took another step toward Sophy and found her all too close. Zounds, but, there was no denying the girl's bold beauty. Her scent was intoxicating. The flame color of her hair lit his senses. The way the long curls framed her creamy complexion was enchanting. His eyes went next to her full cherry lips and then the sure provocativeness of her curves that even in the simple lines of her blue day gown could not disguise. Stop! Mentally, he slapped himself. This was mad. He was no schoolboy to have his head turned by a pretty girl! He managed a casual smile and brought up the small package he had been holding at his side and quietly said, "This is for you."

Sophy's cheeks went red and she backed away from him as though he were giving her a hot iron. "For me? No, no."

"Don't be silly, it's nothing," he hastened to reassure her. Again he gently pushed the prettily wrapped package toward her. "Go on."

She hesitated and then took up the package wrapped in ivory paper and untied the pretty ribbon to uncover one of the loveliest, softest cashmere shawls she had ever seen. It was a beautiful shade of dark blue and was embroidered along its fringes with various blends of blues. She held it up and breathed, "This, this is exquisite. But, I can't, you must not. I do sincerely thank you, but it must have been such an expense." She shook her head and resolutely handed it to him. "I can not accept this."

"I don't agree. I was most thoughtless this morning. I trod your very lovely shawl underfoot in the filth and I am honor bound to replace it. It is no more than that, Miss Egan, I promise you." He grinned conspiratorially. "As to the expense, it was a trifling amount. As it chanced, I was in the company of a very dear friend, my cousin, Amelia. She is a most remarkable woman, and as a result I was witness to some very fine bargaining, upon my word." He smiled warmly at the memory of Amelia's bickering with the shopkeeper over the cost of the shawl.

Sophy was conscious of something that flickered through her. A feeling she could not name. He had been with a female friend. A cousin, a *dear* friend, he had said. An unhabitual feeling of reticence wielded her suddenly and she blushed as she said, "Still . . . but . . ."

"Miss Egan, it is nothing but a shawl for a shawl. Do not make more of it than it really is." There was almost a challenge in those devilish blue eyes. He could see that she felt immensely uncomfortable about accepting what was obviously an expensive gift from a gentleman she scarcely knew. He was curious. Just what would she do? A well bred maid would insist on maintaining the proprieties. At least that had been his experience in the past and his past experiences had been many and varied.

Sophy liked the earl. He had been of immense service on two separate occasions within the last two days. She had no wish to offend and felt to continue to demure just might hurt him. He just might think she was snubbing him because of the reputation he carried. There too, she was beginning to feel foolish. After all, he had a point, did he not? He *had* ruined her shawl.

"Thank you. The shawl is lovely," she said finally holding the pretty thing to herself and inclining her head gracefully. "How silly of me, for although we have only just become acquainted, circumstances have allowed us a quick friendship. If you feel honor bound to replace my shawl, then I too, am honor bound to accept."

"Bravo!" he said with genuine feeling. His mind continued to compliment her. That was certainly well done. She handled herself and the situation with understated social grace. Indeed, the child certainly had style. Yet it was time to go. This female sent warning signals off in his mind. With a civility that bordered on frigidness, he bowed himself off and made good his escape.

Sophy watched him leave. She put the shawl aside on the deep brown velvet sofa and sat to contemplate the Cortland Nabob. He was like no other man she had ever known, that was for certain. She was not sure what to make of him. He was fascinating, yes, but he walked about in a cloud of mystery and she did not like that. Sophy was an open person who appreciated honesty. Secrets and their like only frustrated her, held her at bay. And just what were his secrets? What did he hide behind those brilliant blue eyes? Why was he friendly one moment and then suddenly frozen in ice? Indeed, just who was this Earl of Cortland?

Ten

Johnny Cornes was a hard-working man. He was only nine-and-twenty, but years of struggling had already stooped his shoulders and more often than not, he hung his head as he walked. Once he had made a good living as a home-knitter. Now a new mill had opened, and his work was gone. He had applied for a job tending one of the new machines and had been one of the lucky few taken on, but he received pitiful wages. That was why he had joined the Luddites. He had no education, but, he knew when he was not being given fair treatment by his government. He and the other Luddites only wanted to be treated fairly, that was all.

The problem was the Luddites were resorting to riots. He didn't hold with that and so he would tell them at the meeting later in the week. He glanced round as he entered the tavern and saw the man he was looking for. A facial signal was all that was needed between them. Nothing discernible to the average observer. Johnny needed the new password. It was changed every week. He wouldn't need escort into the forest as some did, for he had grown up near Sherwood and knew it well, but everyone that entered the Luddite ravine would need the password. He took a seat at the bar, ordered a bumper of ale and waited.

The earl had come to this particular tavern for a reason

all his own, but he had not been there more than ten minutes when he realized there were deep doings all around him. His well defined brow went up and he sipped his brew with slow precision. He did not miss the signals that passed between some of the men that entered the tavern. He shook his head, if these men were not more careful, they just might find themselves in serious danger. One table away, sat a small stout man in a peaked wool cap. Out of the corner of his eye, the earl watched as the little man leaned over to adjust his boot and a small black leather notebook dropped out. The fellow glanced round warily as he retrieved his possession and hurriedly shoved it into his inner pocket, thankful that no one had seen it. He was wrong however, for someone had seen. Very little escaped the earl's notice, very little indeed.

The smooth management of the Egan stables was a chore Sophy loved and preferred above all others. However, it was not her only job at Egan Grange. She took special pride in carrying on the tradition her mother had instituted when she had come as a bride to Egan Grange. That was the care and attention given to each and every Egan employee. Sophy discovered in herself a skill as mistress of her father's home, but more than that, she enjoyed knowing that her mother would have been pleased with the results of her efforts. That included giving particular attention to her servants' needs. She would take notice if Cook seemed out of sorts, as she had been last week. It had been the woman's tooth acting up, so Sophy ordered simple meals that the kitchen maid could prepare for the day and sent Cook off with her husband, Jeffries, their head groom, to have the tooth pulled at Mr. Egan's expense. Sophy also made certain that all day-laborers were always sent home to their families with something from the Egan kitchen. But, more than that, Sophy genuinely cared, as her mother had before her. It was not surprising, therefore, that the Egans were loved in Nottingham.

One girl, in particular had come to them only a year ago, when the chambermaid married and moved to another county. Sophy was well pleased with Bessy Cornes, but just a bit concerned about her as well. She was an excellent worker, and Sophy had not a complaint in the world about Bessy, however, more often than not she felt a sure concern when she looked her way.

Sophy had been rummaging about in the attic and to her delight found some considerable yardage of pretty blue cotton. With a sudden notion, she folded it neatly and went in search of Bessy. She found her in the kitchen taking a sip of hot tea and exclaimed, "Oh good. Here you are Bessy. Look what I have found! Isn't this a famous color?" Sophy was always very conscious of other people's pride, for she had a measure of her own and wanted first to set Bess Cornes at ease. She rolled her large green eyes comically and then pulled at her red curls for emphasis. "A famous color for almost anyone else, but not for me. I purchased this some months ago before I realized it was the wrong shade of blue for my coloring."

"Oh, no, miss, ye would look grand in that color," said Bess wide-eyed. Truth was, she thought miss would look beautiful in a feed bag.

Sophy sighed. "You are being kind, but the sorry truth is Papa did not at all care for this shade of blue on me. Up in the attic it went." She put the bundle in Bess's work-roughened hands. "I was just up there and when I found it, I remembered that you mentioned that you enjoy sewing. Bess, there is plenty of yardage here, as well as the matching ribbons that I bought for trimming. You have, I think, enough material to make a Sunday gown for yourself and enough left over to make a dress for each of your lovely little girls." Sophy sighed sweetly. "Such a perfect shade for your fair coloring."

Bessy put a hand to her cheek. "Oh, miss, I couldn't . . ."

"Why not?" Sophy knew just how to guide a situation. "Don't you like this material?"

"Miss, miss, of course I do, but 'tis yers and would make sech a fine morning gown, that it would," Bess replied allowing herself the luxury of running her hand over its softness.

"Papa does not agree. Now, you take this for it is a sin to waste and you wouldn't want me caught in a sin?" Sophy's green eyes twinkled.

Bess took Sophy's hand and dropped a curtsy. "Thank ye, miss. Ye be that good. Thank ye."

"Nonsense," said Sophy who waved this off. But as she watched Bess leave, she sighed, wishing it were possible to do more.

Cook who was well near sixty, considerably more than plump, red-cheeked and whose position in the household was only topped by Nurse, sniffed. She had been at Egan Grange before Sophia was born, and rather thought of Sophy as her own. She was as big-hearted as she was round and sniffed again over the scene she had just witnessed. Then with a wag of her finger she admonished Sophy in a gruff voice to sit herself down. "Ye'll oblige me in this missy, fer wit all yer running around and sech, ye been dropping weight. Yer too long legged to let yerself go like that. Too thin, that whot I told m'Jeffries last night.

So then, ye'll jest sit 'ere wit me and have a spot of tea and one of m'tarts before ye going running off again."

Sophy's eyes were alight as she meekly took up a chair at the long oak table by the fireplace stove and with a laugh said, "Now when, have I ever turned down one of *your* tarts?" Then as a thought struck her she added, "And as to your wonderful tarts, dearest, may I steal a few to take with me up to the Abbey this afternoon?"

Cook's eyes opened wide. She was not quite certain she could have heard her young mistress correctly. "Ye ain't never going up to the Abbey alone?"

Sophy laughed. "I know you think me a hoyden, Cookie, but I am not so lost to propriety as that." Sophy shook her head. "Ned goes with me."

"Humph! And Ned is chaperone enough, is he? Lor' bless ye child. The earl is a bachelor and one hears tell that he has been more wild than most." She put her hands on her hips. "Whot business ye got going up there is more than I can say, but then ye'll be telling me it is none of m'affair."

Sophy threw her arms round Cook's neck. "Never would I say that, my dearest Cookie, especially when I mean to steal a tart or two."

Cookie could not refrain from smiling. She adored Sophy and in the end could refuse her nought. She would, she told herself have a great deal to ask her Jeffries later that day, make no mistake!

In another part of the house, Bess Cornes neatly, lovingly put the blue linen in a cupboard and went about her daily tasks. She was thinking of Johnny. Her job at Egan Grange was a great help. It even allowed her coin enough to give to Aunt Sarah who watched her girls for her all day. But even that hurt Johnny. He felt it was his job to provide, and hers to be home with their children. Her returning to work was what finally drove him to join the brotherhood, and this was something she knew could lead to trouble, serious trouble. What Johnny did was against the law. What if he were caught, sent to prison? But he wouldn't listen. He said a man had to stand up for a man's rights. She frowned as she worked wondering how much deeper her Johnny was being dragged into the Luddite sphere? If only there were some way she could stop him. If only he would listen, and oh, what would he say about the cloth Miss Egan had given her? He would call it charity and demand she give it up. But she wouldn't and then what would he say? She sighed, just what would her Johnny say?

Sophy had dressed with precise care. She wore a decorative top hat of rich brown velvet. The hat was banded with ivory lace that formed a puff bow and flowed down all the way down to the middle of her back. Thick red curls twirled about her fine forehead and at her ears. A high neck ruffle of lace protruded over the narrow lapels of her brown velvet ensemble. The same lace hung in pretty ruffles at her wrist. Ned observed his sister for a long moment as she wielded the reins and chatted idly about her visit with Nathan Walker the other day.

"Oh, so that explains it," grinned Ned.

"Explains what, brat?" Sophy knew from his look that he meant to be outrageous.

"Why you are dressed to the nines!" snorted Ned wickedly.

Sophy was busy at that moment turning their carriage horse onto the Cortland Abbey drive. The gates were open and without stopping at the old stone gatehouse, she drove the gig slowly up the tree lined winding driveway. Surprised by this remark she glanced ruefully at her young brother. "Dressed to the nines, indeed. What, my lad, is that supposed to mean?"

"Well, Nathan Walker will be up at the Abbey." Ned laughed. "So what do you think it means, sis. I am eleven, after all, and know what is toward."

She pulled a face at him. "Don't be absurd."

His expression turned suddenly serious. "The thing is, Soph, I wish you didn't like *him* so much."

She was surprised. "Neddy, Don't *you* like Nathan?"

Ned shrugged. "Oh, I suppose he is a decent enough chap, but Soph, he won't do for you."

"Wouldn't he?" she laughed. "And why not, halfling?"

He grinned. "Told you. I'm eleven, not a baby. Soph, remember when we went for a ride together two summers ago? I do. You and I were itching to run. Bouncer was throwing his head around. Walker just prosed on and on and then went through the gate when you jumped the wall. Through the gate, Soph!" He shook his head with sad disbelief. "Now, Soph, you like to run and jump, run and jump, that's what you like."

"Is that how you see it?" Soph was very much amused by this new side of her young brother. She had not suspected him of such mature perceptions. "And there *are* times when one should not jump a horse."

"But that ain't the point sis. We were out for a ride, a ride, Soph. And his horse was sound." He sighed. "The thing is, in the end Nathan Walker will bore you to tears."

"Odious boy," laughed Sophy. "That is a terrible thing to say."

He shrugged his shoulders. "No lie, though."

She shook her head. "I think you are out of your depth, Ned Egan."

"Now you are either too lovesick to see, Cookie says that happens to women more often than not, or you are pitching your gammon at me." He eyed her gravely. "I heard Nathan Walker say to Papa that he thinks women are loveliest when they are sitting at their stitchery."

"Ned, you never did?" ejaculated Sophy stopping the gig to look at him full.

"Well, and I did." He eyed her. "Soph, you don't stitch and *I* like you just the way you are—riding to hounds first flight, wearing britches, oh, all the sort of things you do. Walker is nought but, but, dull sport, much like Papa." This last was said on a bitter note and he looked away.

Sophy was taken aback. She had not realized just how dissatisfied Ned was with their father. Uncertain of just what to say to this, she kept silent for a space and then decided to take the conversation to lighter ground for the moment. "So, my brother the sage has spoken," teased Sophy pinching his nose with her soft kid gloved hand.

He pulled away sharply and retorted on a pugnacious note, "Make light of it, but mark me tis something I know."

Sophy laughed. "Well, I'll have you know that I am not dressed to the nines as you put it for Mr. Walker. *Whenever* I dress, I dress to the nines."

"Ha!" retorted her brother relenting with a half smile.

Cortland Abbey was now in full sight as Sophy drove their open gig past an army of men working the estate's grassy park. A dusting of lime covered the freshly cut grass. Evergreens were being trimmed and shaped.

Sophy exclaimed appreciatively, "Oh, look Neddy, the grounds will be magnificent when the earl is done."

"Aye." He regarded his sister thoughtfully. "Do you think the earl misses India?"

"Well, I don't know. I think he missed England while he was there, but 'tis difficult to say. We don't really know him well enough."

"It's odd, Soph," he said smiling. "It feels as though we have been friends with him forever."

It was at that moment that the earl stepped out from behind a huge overgrown evergreen, shovel in hand. He was in his shirtsleeves, and there was a boyish grin on his handsome features. Indeed, at that moment, Sophy felt she had known him a great deal longer than she had.

Eleven

"Welcome!" The earl called, his blue eyes smiling, then he turned and spoke softly to a nearby lackey who immediately went to hold the cob horse steady as Sophy put up the brake.

Ned was already scrambling out of the open carriage and coming round to help his sister, but the earl was there before him and lightly held her trim waist as he saw her easily to the ground.

"Forgive us. No doubt we have chosen a bad time to descend upon you." Sophy hoped her voice didn't sound as shaky to him as it did to her.

"Nonsense, that is if you don't mind finding me in all my dirt? I learned the art of gardening when I was in India and grew to love puttering with plants." He smiled warmly, "It is a very soothing occupation."

"Oh, yes, indeed, I am always in the garden with my roses, my flowers, and my vegetables. I take a great deal of pleasure in growing them myself, much to Nurse's dismay," beamed Sophy happily. "I must say the grounds are looking splendid."

"Are those buildings up there all stables?" Ned interjected, as he had little interest in their talk of dirt and vegetables.

"Yes, for the most part they are made of twelfth century

rough hewn stone as is most of the Abbey. The smaller
building on the left of the barn is the wellhouse. I've had
that restored into working order. You might like to have
a look at the treadwheel inside that building. Donkeys are
used to turn its wheel." The earl smiled and then gently
ruffled Ned's unruly head of red hair. "And good afternoon to you, scamp."

Ned grinned sheepishly. "Churlish manners, eh? I *am*
sorry. I'm a shocking fellow."

"Ho! Listen to this lad. I am not in my dotage and do
not fall for such bait." The earl eyed Sophy playfully. "I
have no doubt he has acquired his appealing charm at
your skirt hem?"

Sophy's green eyes twinkled. "Have you no doubt? You
should. For Papa tells me I am as much hoyden as Ned
is a veritable devil."

The earl laughed and forgetting his resolve to keep Sophy at a distance, he took her gloved hand and audaciously
slid it through his bent arm. "Come, we'll walk up to the
stables first, that is," he directed a mockingly inquiring
eye at Ned, "if it suits Master Egan?"

"That it does. How many paddocks have you for your
bloods?"

"We've only managed to enclose three paddocks with
fencing, but they are two acres each. There is a smaller
stud paddock just outside the barn and of course, the large
five-acre field has its original fencing which will do for
now."

"By Jove, I should think so." Ned was obviously impressed. "We have only Princess as a brood mare, though
I plan to have another as well, when I am old enough to
take over the stable management." He grinned sideways
at his sister. "Soph does a bang up job of it, but I should

like to put out some race horses and enter them at the Derby." He puzzled at the earl. "Do your mares graze together, then?"

"Yes. We have four brood mares and they do well together in one paddock. We rotate the remaining horses and it serves for now."

"Zounds!" breathed Ned, awed. "How many horses *do* you have?"

"Ned!" objected his sister who had until this moment been much impressed with her brother's mature conversation. He had always had a love of horses and horse management.

The earl smiled and waved off her objection. "We have a few. And something else I brought back from India. Peacocks. There are two, a male and a female. They roam around freely in the Abbey's enclosed courtyard garden."

"Peacocks?" Ned cried as his face lit up, once more the little boy. "Famous! Soph, did you hear that? Peacocks!" His club foot prevented him from running toward the stables and inner courtyard to observe all these wonders, but unconscious of his infirmity, he did hurry up the sloped walking path ahead.

Sophy had been listening to their conversation, but it sounded as though it were coming from a long distance away. Peacocks? Yes. "Peacocks. How very fascinating," was what she thought she had mumbled. She felt encased in fairy dust. Why was that? Because she was aware, all too titillatingly aware of her hand resting on his strong, hard arm just inside his bent elbow. It felt so improper, but of course, it was not, at least, she didn't think it was. Her heart was beating so very wildly and her cheeks were burning. She was conscious, all too conscious of his handsome profile, though she didn't dare look up at him. She was conscious of his magnetism, of the size of his broad shoulders, of his height.

He stopped to point out the horseshoe flower bed his gardeners had designed at the crest of the slope just below the central stable. It was ablaze with yellow daffodils and its edging all around was alive with perfectly formed violets.

Sophy shook off her wayward sensations and managed to respond suitably, saying that the daffodils were lovely.

Ned had reached the stone archway to the stable courtyard and turned to urge them to hurry. "What are you two doing? Come on!"

Sophy laughed. "We *are* coming you incorrigible rascal. We simply are not as fast as you!"

"Go on," called the earl. "You may start without us and if you encounter a grizzled old Irishman named Daniel, you may tell him I have given you the run of the place. I mean to detour your sister a moment and show her the finest view in all of Nottingham!"

"A view?" said Ned in a tone that indicated a very poor opinion of this occupation. He shrugged and hurried through the archway where he very promptly encountered Daniel.

There were a set of stone steps laid neatly in the freshly cut grass, just before and to the left of the stone archway Ned had just passed through. The earl shifted his hold on Sophy by imperceptibly removing his arm from her fingers to take hold of her elbow and direct her up these steps.

As they climbed, Sophy laughed and started to count, "Faith! I've counted fourteen already and I did not even start at the first steps. How high does this take us?"

He grinned. "You'll see and there are seventy-two steps in total."

"Never say so! Why?"

"The Abbey was originally built like a fortress. We once had a stone keep at the top of this rise. It was used as a lookout in the early Norman days. Richard of Cortland, who was the second earl, took down the walls of the keep." He beamed roguishly. "However, he was a bit of a rake. He would bring his lady loves up here with the hope that they would fall exhausted into his arms. If that failed, he relied on the view to create the mood."

Sophy eyed him quizzically for she was already out of breath and she could see there was still a climb ahead of them. "Unless he carried his women to the top, I can well imagine they might be too exhausted to resist his advances!"

He laughed. "The story was that Richard was quite a gentleman, he never took what wasn't fairly offered." The earl stopped then and looked into her green eyes flirtatiously. "It is one of the things I liked in my ancestor." He allowed her to catch her breath and turned away then to point to their far right. "See there, that stretch of ground? Another ancestor built those ramparts in the sixteenth century."

"Faith, I have never seen anything like that. Imagine, Egan is only a few miles away and I never even knew. I've read about the use of ramparts in the sixteenth century, but look how well disguised these are!"

"Indeed, they were used as a highly efficient defense against artillery. It would be virtually impossible to carry cannon over each roll to get within range of the Abbey. The landscaping was actually installed some years later as the need of ramparts became obsolete." He grinned wickedly then. "However, I found a great many uses for them as a boy at play. When I took on some years and discovered the wonders of the gentler sex, I discovered an entirely different manner in which to use them." Tongue in cheek he started the climb again.

Sophy shook her head as she cocked a half smile his way, "No doubt, you are much in the image of your notorious Richard of Cortland."

He laughed. "As a matter of fact, there is a portrait of Richard in the Great Hall. You may decide for yourself."

"I should like to see his portrait," Sophy giggled. "I am beginning to think he was something of a Blackbeard who did away with the least favorite of his women by tricking them into making this climb in the hopes of some obscure view. View? Do I care for a view when my lungs are in danger of exploding?" Her smile belied the words. "I already counted fifty steps, my lord." She reached out then to detain him for another resting spell. She felt slightly flushed. "A moment, my lord."

He grinned. "I thought you would never ask . . ."

"I suppose I am not as fit as I thought myself. My word, this is a climb!" She looked about herself. "It is a shame your Richard took down the keep. It was a part of history."

"It was in ruins." He regarded her with a mock sorrow as he added, "And as it turned out, Richard was shot through the heart."

"Oh, how very sad," said Sophy, her eyes teasing.

"Indeed. A tragedy. It happened when a neighbor's granddaughter came to visit—"

"Her grandfather shot him?" Sophy interrupted in shocked accents.

He grinned and flicked her nose, "No, she did, with

cupid's arrow. He got married, settled down with a brood of noisy brats, and vanished into domestic bliss."

Sophy giggled. "I like that."

His blue eyes glittered. " 'Tis an odd thing, but when my father recounted the story of Richard's life to me I rather liked the happy ending the best. Come along now, your rest is over!"

At the top of the stairs he led her to a stone parapet, and pointed out various things of interest. "And there, to the north, are the ruins of the Cistercian Monastery. After the Dissolution, the stones were used to add extensively to the house, and it was then that the place became known as Cortland Abbey." He took her hand. "We had best go down." He liked the feel of her hand in his as he pulled her along, and he was aware of a thrill as the sound of her carefree laughter bounced about in his mind. There was time enough to put her at a distance, and no reason at all why he should not enjoy the pleasure of her delightful company for the moment.

Ned was blissfully running about the stables with Daniel in tow. He asked question upon question, scarcely waited for the answers and then joyfully found himself in the well-house. This proved to be the find of the day and nothing would do for him, but to talk poor Daniel into hitching up two mules to set the thing in motion.

It was during this fascinating experience that Nathan Walker entered in search of the earl. "Young Ned," Walker said with some surprise. "Where did you spring from?"

"The earl invited us," answered Ned almost defiantly.

Nathan Walker laughed and attempted to give the boy a friendly pat on his head. Ned pulled out of range. Walker smiled indulgently. "I did not mean to imply that you were here without an invitation." He looked about for Sophia. When he had asked her to stop by the Abbey to view his architectural achievement, he had not expected her to take up the invitation so quickly. He had expected that she would display a very proper demureness and allow at least a day or two to pass before showing herself at the Abbey. However, he knew Sophy had always been a high spirited female. That was the fault of her father's free hand. She was allowed far too much license. Then too, Ned had no doubt dragged her here to explore the Abbey. The lad was spoiled and pampered all because of his infirmity. "Indeed, Ned, I was hoping you and your sister would drop by." He looked round casually. "And where is your sister? I assume you came up together?"

"She went with the earl to have a look at some view or other," said Ned wishing Walker at Jericho.

"Really?" Nathan returned in some surprise. He did not like the sound of that. Nathan Walker had spent two busy years in London. During that time, he had developed quite a reputation as a very talented architect. In the last few months before he had returned to Nottingham to work on the Abbey renovations, he had looked about for a wife and found society's debutantes sadly lacking. Either they were hanging out for a title and great wealth, or were not to his taste.

Then he had visited Sophia. His eyes lit up when he surveyed her and he felt a certain flutter in his chest. He'd discovered that the pretty hoyden of a girl had developed into quite an extraordinarily beautiful woman. Though she had not grown out of her high spirits, he found her style, her grace, her general air of assurance most charming. She was not a restful female, and her sauciness was not precisely what he wanted in a woman, but he sensed a sure maturity beneath it all that he felt he was capable of molding and shaping into the type of wife he would expect her to be. She was still an ingenue, and must be protected from the likes of the Cortland Nabob! Going off to see the view alone, indeed!

"Daniel and I were about to set the treadwheel in motion. Would you like to watch?" Ned offered politely.

"No, no. I think I will just . . . er see if I can find the earl, thank you." Nathan Walker hurried off to have a quick survey of the grounds.

Sophy laughed when she reached the bottom step and as she turned to give a saucy glance to the earl, put a supporting hand to her midriff and declared, "Faith, but coming down was such a very easy feat compared to the trip up!" She waved off the objection he was about to utter and begrudgingly said with a warm smile, "But well worth it, my lord. It *is* a spectacular view. Why, you can see all of the county!" Sophy's green eyes glittered then with a tease as she amiably added, "Indeed, I envy you the view, but not, my lord, the climb." She shook her head, and then wagged a reproving finger at him as he chuckled in response to her banter. "I will have you know, my lord, that I walk a good three miles a day, perhaps even more than that, and I ride. I have never considered myself a missish sort, and yet I found that climb completely exhausting. I think I shall immediately go home."

He grinned. "No, no, there are the remaining grounds, the bowling green, the old chapel, the house, the domestic buildings . . ."

"Wicked man. All today?" Sophy returned teasingly.

"Ah, there you are, my lord," called Nathan Walker as he waved and walked toward them.

"Nathan, thank goodness. You are here to rescue me," cried Sophy, mockingly dramatic. She was surprised to see the sudden cloud cover Walker's face.

"Rest easy," said the earl as the laughter in his blue eyes died. "I believe Miss Egan is only jesting."

"I am not. Behold, the Demon of Cortland, exercising his guests to the death," laughed Sophy. However, she quickly witnessed the distress on Walker's face and laughed deliciously. "No, no Nathan, you needn't fret it. I really am at play, honestly."

Walker smiled. "When are you not?" He then looked at the earl. "You are needed at the chapel. The special windows you ordered have arrived, but as I was not with you in London when you purchased them, I could not now give my approval."

The earl's eyes flickered, but he inclined his head with a smile, "Of course." He turned to Sophy and he found he couldn't stop himself from uttering the next words; they came with an apologetic smile. "I have a notion you just might like."

"And what might that be, my lord?"

"My mother had an older sister. Suffice it to say that we are close. When all the world was ready to believe the worst of me, she did not. On blind faith. At any rate, my aunt means to set herself up in my home and substantiate me in society, at least that is what she wrote." He grinned boyishly.

Sophy laughed. "Substantiate you? I think you do that very well for yourself, my lord. But it will be nice to have her with you, I am sure."

He eyed Sophia for a moment. "Thank you, though

you are off the mark." He shrugged. "For myself, I care little for society's opinions, however I am bound by honor and affection to care for my aunt's concerns." He touched Sophy's elbow as though drawing her to himself. "We digress. I thought you and Ned might enjoy a visit to the Abbey when my aunt is established here, which should be any day now if I know Aunt Lucinda." He arched a comical brow. "At any rate, that would allow me to offer you the hospitalities of my home and we could explore at leisure."

Walker did not like this suggestion and frowned as he hurried to interject, "If it is more convenient, Miss Egan could continue her tour now with me as her guide?"

Miss Egan's sense of humor elicited her response. "I think I shall make good my escape now and return when Aunt Lucinda is about to curb all this gadding about through keeps and ramparts and such!"

Nathan Walker was annoyed, but he politely inclined his head. "As you wish, Sophia."

She could see that he was offended, but Ned appeared at that exact moment, hobbling toward them his face flushed with excitement as he advised the Earl, "You've a bang up set up here, my lord, bang up!"

"High praise, indeed, scamp! It is up to you to make your sister bring you back, eh?" He turned to Sophy. "I am sorry. I must not keep the masons waiting any longer."

She watched him go and turned to Ned, "Come on, Neddy, it is getting late, and I did want to be home to have tea with Papa."

"Oh, but . . ." complained Ned.

Sophy started walking toward the courtyard where her open gig and cob horse had been taken by one of Cortland's young grooms. The boy saw them coming and immediately went to the cob's head to hold him steady.

Walker wielded himself in place so that he was able to hand Sophy into the carriage saying, "I am sorry I was not about when you arrived. I would have enjoyed taking you through parts of the Abbey to show you the changes we have made."

"Indeed, I am sorry as well," smiled Sophy kindly. He was an old and dear friend, but, he had never displayed any romantic interest in her before. She was just a bit surprised to see her light words had mollified him. She felt a twinge of something she could not name, and the notion hit her that here was a stranger. As a girl, she had seen a knight in shining armor when she had looked his way. Now? Now, she saw a man, and he was so much more staid than she had remembered.

A moment later they had taken their leave and Sophy was slowly driving her carriage down the long winding front drive. She did not realize that Nathan Walker stood a long time watching her through narrowed, thoughtful eyes. Nor did she know that from another divide of Cortland the Earl was watching her back, and that a frown had descended over his features.

Twelve

Bessy had been right. Her Johnny became very agitated when she showed him the lovely material Miss Egan had given to her. He yanked it from her hands and angrily threw the neat bundle across the small room saying they wouldn't take charity.

She had scurried to the floor and tenderly picked up the blue cloth, gently brushing off any floor dust and eyed him sadly, her lips forming a stubborn pout. "You're turning mean, John Cornes, and that is a truth!"

Guilt rushed over him in a wave and he threw up his hands. "Keep the damn stuff. 'Tis only, I should be the one giving it to ye, darlin'." He hit his chest as he spat out the words and turned on his heel. He left their small cottage in a cloud of misery, stampeding past his two little girls as though they were not there.

As he walked the four miles towards Sherwood Forest, his shoulders sagged and visions of the scene he had just left behind began to haunt him. He needed help. The mill was turning him into a monster without hope. Hope? It blossomed in the woods when the brotherhood all gathered and they listened to the man they knew only as King Ludd. He was gentry, at least, he sounded as though he were. He always wore a hood and came and went like the wind. He just seemed to appear and then vanish like magic.

Ludd had written a letter, a warning of sorts to the House of Lords. He had read it to the brotherhood at their last meeting, and inspired, they had rallied and cheered him on with pure trust and confidence. He had written about their desperation. He had stood up to their all powerful government and told the demi-gods of London about the precarious working and living conditions of the English factory workers and of the English weavers. He was their voice, and he wasn't afraid to tell the government about his peoples' ever growing discontent in Nottingham and even further north. Now, it was rumored that King Ludd had received word regarding their impassioned plea. Time would tell whether Johnny went to the mill to work tomorrow or took up arms with his Luddite brothers.

Sophy's attention had wandered during dinner with her father and Ned. It didn't seem to matter as both her male relatives seemed more than usually preoccupied as well. She could see that Ned's attitude toward their father was most distant. This troubled Sophy and she made a mental resolve to do something about it first thing in the morning. When she was fresh.

Saying good-night to her father once dinner was finished, she went off to Ned's room where he was concentrating on a new sketch. He shoved it in her face and demanded her honest opinion. Sophy cooed at once. It was an excellent sketch of his new colt, Intrepid. "Neddy, you are a wonderful artist, truly."

He hugged her fiercely around her trim waist and shut

his eyes as he spoke with intensity, "I'm glad you're here Soph."

She touched his cheek. "I am too, my little man. Go on, you may continue with your sketching if you like. I am going to my room with this book and mean to rest my weary bones."

Once in her room, she settled in her most comfortable chair by her balcony window. There was a wonderful fire burning in the small marble framed fireplace. A branch of candles on a side table at her elbow gave off additional light, but Sophy couldn't read. The words seemed to blur and fade into a haze. Her mind drifted into a jumble of thoughts that ended in a picture, a very vivid picture of the Earl of Cortland.

Stop! You are allowing yourself to behave like a silly schoolgirl. She bit her lip and glanced outside for she had not drawn the drapes yet. A nearly full moon demanded attention in a sky ablaze with stars. Such a view, she thought, and immediately his boyish grin came to mind and punctuated the moment. How delightful he had been that afternoon when he had taken her up that literally breathtaking climb, for an incredible view of all of Nottinghamshire. He had been genuine and open, almost childlike, sharing a favorite plaything with a friend. Sophy had liked him at once, but, more than that, she knew she was very drawn to him. Well, there was no great wonder in that. She smiled for she was forever honest with herself. He was the very broth of a man, surely different than anyone she had ever known. He was virile, handsome, tall, built like a mountain and had such laughing beautiful blue eyes. And he was certainly out of her reach. She was sure he found her no more than an ordinary country girl. That was all she was, after all. He on the other hand, was well traveled, sophisticated, self-assured, somewhat older. Twelve, nearly thirteen years older in fact! She sighed. And there was no doubt in her mind that he was besieged by beautiful, fashionable women from all sides. She shook her head and decided that he had his pick of women and would never think twice about her.

This very naturally spoiled the beauty of the moment and brought a frown to her dark winged brows. However, her mood was interrupted by a sudden knock sounding at her door. She called out a welcome as she turned in her chair.

Ned burst in on her and ran to her window, his finger to his lips. She opened her green eyes wide and started to question his very odd behavior, but he pulled a face at her and whispered a definite warning, "Shhhhh." He then immediately extinguished her candles, and returned to wrap himself in her velvet drapes. Then he said, "Come here, Soph, and look!"

Sophy was more than astonished at his odd behavior. However, he was a boy and given to antics. She smiled and humored him by taking a place just behind him to peek out her window and inquire, "What shall I look at, Neddy?"

"Don't you see it?" he asked in tones of exasperation, "There, skirting across the lawns toward Cortland woods."

"See what?" Sophy was now looking in earnest.

"The *light* Soph, from a lantern! Sophy, *someone is out there!*"

Harry was driving his open gig. Beside him sat Oscar and both were deep in thought. They were on their way to town to attend a meeting called by the local magistrate.

Harry felt it was his duty as a landowner, though he was only twenty-one years old, to present himself and offer his opinion and advice. In this frame of mind, he demanded that Oscar accompany him as his guest.

Oscar's first, second and last reaction to this invitation, was to respectfully, but happily, decline. Harry's heavy hand won out in the end. The thing was that both Harry and Oscar had no doubt whatsoever about what the discussion at the meeting would entail. They were fully aware that there was a growing unrest in town, and that the reigning gentry were sure it was related to the Luddite movement.

News of machine smashing further North had headlined the *Chronicle* the other morning. Rumors of impending riots in their own mills and factories were a very real possibility. However, as for young Harry Ingram and his friend, Oscar Bently, their very real sympathies were with the desperate laborers. They both had household servants that had been with them since childhood, and these employees had relatives suffering from the conditions they endured in the local mills. Harry and Oscar were patriotic Englishmen and these were their fellow hardworking Englishmen in dire straits. However, they knew their views were not popular and would not be welcome this night.

Harry glanced toward Egan Grange as they turned off the smaller country road that emptied from his estate drive and he stopped his horse to say, "What the deuce?"

"What?"

"Look there, moving toward Sherwood. A lantern light. I swear it is!"

"By Jove! Damn, if it isn't?" Oscar considered the possibilities and sighed, "It's Neddy, I suppose on one of his larks."

"Zounds, that lad is a handful." Harry grinned. "Lively, but he is a good lad." He made a clicking sound to his horse. "The thing is, Oscar, with all the queer disquiet in Sherwood he could get hurt."

"Aye," nodded his friend.

"Well, Sophy needs some help with that one," announced Harry with resignation. "Look here. When we are done with this argle-bargle meeting tonight, you spend the night. We'll go visit with Sophy first thing in the morning. What say you?"

"Aye, good notion, that," agreed Oscar who had already imbibed a bottle of wine with Harry at dinner, and meant to down a few more glasses of the same before the dreaded meeting progressed too deep.

"Soph, come on. We can take a short-cut through the kitchen and follow him," said Ned taking her hand and pulling her toward the door.

"No Ned, this is silly. It could be anyone . . ." the words sounded hollow even to herself. The day servants had already left the grounds hours ago. She could not think of any of their live-in people who would be wandering about at this hour, especially in the direction of Cortland Wood? "Besides, I don't have my shoes on!"

"Put them on as we go. Come on Soph, this isn't the first time I've seen someone lurking about at night!"

Sophy bent to grab her half boots out of her wardrobe cabinet and with only her stockings on her feet, hurried after him. "What do you mean this isn't the first time, Edward Egan?" She pulled at his hair as he rushed down the stairs. "Ned, have you actually seen someone with a lantern light running about our grounds before and not said a word to me or to Papa?"

"Shhh. Papa will hear you. He is still awake." Ned pointed to the shaft of light shining beneath their father's door. "Yes, last week, but I didn't think much about it then."

They reached the bottom step and Sophy hopped along as she pulled on one boot and then the other. They finally reached the dark regions of the kitchen where they carefully picked their way to the back door. Outside, Sophy hugged herself for it was cool and she hadn't even her shawl.

"There," whispered Ned excitedly as he pointed to the light skimming along the edge of the woods some two hundred feet ahead of them. "There he goes, Soph. He is moving slow and still headed in the direction of Cortland Wood." He started to hobble off saying, "Soph, please, we have to catch up if we are not to lose him. I can't run as fast as you, so you go ahead, do."

Sophy was now as curious as she was concerned. Just what was going on here? Were the Luddites using Egan Grange to get to Sherwood undetected? Was that what was happening? "Right then love, stay as close as you can to me." On these words she took off, her skirts in her hand.

Thirteen

The earl rode his large black hunter down the main pike toward Cortland. Dinner with Amelia and Arthur, two of his dearest, closest friends proved to be an event he had scarcely been able to participate in with any measure of genuine interest. This was not due to poor spirits or ill humor, because, in fact, he was in the best of good moods. Yet, he knew himself engulfed in a fog. His mind kept wandering in spite of his attempt to get a hold of the present. He found himself constantly reliving the pleasurable events of the day.

However, he had managed to interject a word here and there into the conversation at hand, laugh at all the appropriate times and happily was convinced they did not notice the fact that he was present in body only. He was saved after dinner by Amelia, who had decided to announce the fact to both her husband and their best friend that she was with child!

After much rallying, congratulations and lively banter, the earl made good his escape, leaving the happy couple to cuddle and coo over their delightful destiny. He was sincerely happy for them, as he loved them dearly, but he was glad to be on his horse, he was glad for the solitude, and he was glad to be on his way home.

He wanted to think. He wanted to banish the picture of

Sophy's laughing green eyes twinkling at him. He wanted to vanquish the desire to kiss her cherry lips. He damned himself for hearing still the sound of her giggle tickling his senses. He wished he had not taken her up that climb to the top of the ridge. He wished he had not touched her hand. Devil a bit! He had to forget this absurdity, he berated himself. *She is an enchanting beauty, but, she is not for you. What would she want with a roué, a tarnished rogue, like yourself. Damnation, what do you want with such an ingenue as she? You would no doubt be heartily bored after a week in her company. Forget her flaming ringlets and her emerald eyes. Besides, it is obvious she and Nathan Walker mean to make a match of it. Walker was in a state today because you took her off, and she was no doubt pleased to make him jealous? That's what the female likes to do, is it not?*

Suddenly the elevation of his spirits plummeted and with a sigh, he decided to take a short-cut through one of his tenant farmers' pastures. The moon and the bright stars were in a cloudless sky and helped light his way. He reached the edge of the woods that divided Cortland Abbey, Egan Grange and Sherwood Forest. There he saw a bobbing light.

He quieted his horse, who saw the same and shied away in some nervous fright, and then waited, as he narrowed his eyes and attempted to discern the outline of the form carrying the oversized lantern. The earl frowned for if it were a man, he was of no great size. Then he grimaced to himself as the next notion suggested that it might be young Ned out on a wild lark. The dark shape holding the lantern moved again, and the earl shook his head. This was not Ned, for the person walked sound. Frowning he urged his horse forward at a slow pace directly into the field, hoping he and his horse were quiet enough. There was just enough of a breeze rustling the tall rye grass to disguise the sound of his movements. Just what was going on here was a question he was now determined to find an answer for. It then flickered logically that perhaps this was no more than some wretched poacher. No doubt he only meant to check his traps. If so, the earl wanted the man's measure for apparently he was headed for Cortland land. If this were the case, the fellow deserved a proper welcome! Quietly he squeezed his horse's flanks and sent him galloping easily through the tall grass across the entire field.

Suddenly, the figure holding the lantern stopped dead. It turned then and dove into the thick of the woods. The earl cursed softly to himself, wondering if the blasted fellow had seen or heard him coming. It took only a moment to reach the edge of the thicket and then he was jumping to the ground to hurriedly tether his black steed to a nearby branch.

A sure sound at his broad back sent his hand carefully up to his saddle. All at once he spun round sharply, his body bent low on his knees, as he brought up his horse pistol in his hand to level a command.

"Stand easy now!" There could be no doubt to anyone listening to the sound of his voice that he would brook no argument.

"If you like, but then we shall lose him," Sophy answered as she attempted to catch her breath.

"Sophy . . . Miss Egan, what are you doing here?" He had dropped his arm immediately and moved quickly to take her shoulder in a protective stance.

"Never mind that. Look, I can just make out the light. We must hurry." She was moving into the woods.

The earl held her arm, detaining her, but Ned, out of

breath arrived at that moment to complain as he rushed the thicket, "You are letting him get away. Come on, we have to follow!"

Sophy pulled out of the earl's hold as she ran into the woods and moved in the direction of the bobbing light. The earl was on her immediately and putting her almost roughly at his back. "I, not *we,* will take up this chase. You and the halfling here would be better served if you were safely home and in your beds!" He was already moving quickly, weaving deftly through the brush and trees even as he spoke.

"Safe in our beds?" Sophy nearly snorted, but she never broke her stride as she hurried after him. Her brother skipped behind her, thinking that the earl had not heard the last of this issue, for he knew his sister well. It only took a moment for Sophy's seething to overflow. "Do you know, I had not suspected you capable of saying such an unhandsome thing!"

The earl looked over his shoulder much amused to see Sophy block her face with her arm as she scrambled through the heavy brush after him. "Ah, no doubt you would find me more acceptable if I did not try and protect you and your brother?" There was a softness in his voice that did manage to reach her frazzled nerves and soothed.

He could almost see her face as she begrudgingly allowed the merit of his argument. "I am not going to argue the point with you now. But be forewarned that when next we have a moment, this is a subject we must explore." She pulled her skirt from a prickly bush. "For the time being, you lead, we do not at all object to following you!" Sophy smiled sweetly in the darkness and though he could not see the smile he heard all too well the stubborn edge to her voice.

The earl turned round and grinned. "Come on then, if you can keep up."

"You keep up with *him,* we'll keep up with you, my lord," Sophy retorted, though she thought, in fact, that her lungs and legs might just give out if they maintained this pace any longer. Poor Ned was some distance behind her.

"What the . . . ? He is *gone!*" hissed the earl in some chagrin. "I don't understand this? I just had the blasted light in my sights. Could he have put it out?"

They were back to back, standing still and looking round. "That's what he has done. He must have heard us and extinguished the lantern. It's our fault for making so much noise." Sophy groaned.

"What has happened?" Ned was out of breath as he reached them. His club foot had been sadly taxed on this outing. He had bumped and stubbed it several times in the dark against rocks and tree stumps, and he was tired, but still ready for more. "Never say we have lost him?"

"I am sorry, scamp, it looks that way," whispered the earl.

"The question is, just who is he and what does he think he is doing cutting across Egan to get to Cortland, for we *are* on your land are we not, my lord?" Sophy asked thoughtfully.

"That is just it. We are standing in Cortland Woods, but we do border Sherwood Forest just here. He could have slinked into Sherwood easily enough without my seeing him once he put his lantern out, I suppose." The earl shrugged, "However, he will have a difficult time checking his traps without light."

"Checking his traps?" Sophy repeated doubtfully. "You think he might be a poacher?" She shook her head. "Why would a poacher enter the woods in such a roundabout way?"

"If he was a poacher, he was like none I've ever encountered," scoffed young Ned.

The earl grinned. "Well, Master Egan, what do you think is this fellow's ken?"

It was Ned's turn to grin and sheepishly reply, "Well, I don't quite have a theory."

"Don't you? Very well, you may have one by tomorrow. For now, I mean to escort you two home where you may both give it some thought." He smiled at Sophy and smoothed her ruffled feathers by adding, "Perhaps, in the light of day, an investigation here may prove fruitful, if you two would care to join me tomorrow?"

"Famous!" cried Ned, his spirits picking up at once.

Sophy knew he was making a peace offering and liked him for it. "Done." she said simply. "What time shall we meet?"

"After Ned's lessons. Then you may invite me back to Egan to enjoy a high tea with you."

Sophy blushed in the darkness as she nodded her head and managed to say that she thought this was a most workable notion.

Fourteen

Sophy sat up in bed and stretched. It was a glorious spring morning. Outside her balcony window birds fluttered and chirped prettily. She sank back against her pillows and shut her eyes. Dreamily she brought back to mind their walk home with the earl last evening.

Ned had been almost skipping with excitement, questions, and speculations when he suddenly remembered that he had not had his full tour at the Abbey and missed meeting the earl's peacocks.

The earl laughed and looked at Sophy. "I am afraid you must apply to your sister then to bring you back, and soon."

She arched a brow. "Never say Aunt Lucinda has arrived already?"

"Ah, alas, no. But I do expect she shall arrive any day now." All this while his hand had been beneath her elbow, it slipped now further up her arm.

She gently moved out of his hold, but her eyes twinkled as she smiled to say, *"I* think we shall await your aunt's arrival before we visit."

He laughed, but Ned interrupted. "Soph." He had been patiently awaiting the outcome of the banter between the earl and his sister. They were smiling, they seemed to like each other and he did not see why they had to wait for

this aunt of the earl's to arrive before they could pay another visit to the Abbey. He kicked at the grass he was
walking through and voiced another objection, "It isn't
fair."

However, his sister wasn't quite listening to him at that
particular moment. She was looking up at the earl's handsome face as his laughing eyes made her smile in return.
He was whispering softly to her, "What then, Miss Egan?
Don't you trust me?"

"Should I, my lord? Tell me true, should I?" She was
only teasing and had no idea he would be so very hurt,
but he was.

All at once, his expression turned grave and he pulled
up to his full height. "Perhaps not," he answered and there
again was the sound of a hurt boy in the tone. It bothered
her.

Well, that was last night. Now it was morning. Suddenly
Sophy jumped up, a beaming smile on her face. It was
too beautiful to stay in bed. She had an awful lot to do
today before she and Ned would be free to meet with the
earl.

Mr. Harcot was announced and the earl looked up from
the pile of paperwork on his huge, gothic desk to smile,
push his chair back and go forward to warmly greet his
young solicitor.

"Good morning, sir." The earl indicated an ornately
carved chair beside his desk. "Please make yourself as
comfortable as you can on that thing. I fear I unwisely
gave in to whimsy when I allowed myself to keep it. There
isn't very much to choose from in the way of furniture
here. I've left that to last. I will ring for coffee." He did

this and returned to take up his oversized dark leather winged chair behind his desk.

"Thank you, my lord. Things are progressing rapidly here. I am glad. My father tells me that your father would have been pleased."

The earl inclined his head. "Yes, I think so." He grinned. "At least it pleases me to think so. Now, what have you for me?"

"I am happy to advise you that we have discovered who owns the tract of land you are interested in purchasing," Harcot answered him, taking out a document from his inner pocket and placing it on the desk.

The earl's brow went up. "That was quick."

"It proved to be a simple task of record searching," Harcot answered, but the truth of it was, he was most pleased with himself for he had not given the work to one of their clerks. He had searched out the information himself.

"I thank you, sir, for I am not *just* interested in this parcel of land. It is more, much more. You see, that land would now still be Cortland land had my brother not wantonly gambled it off." The earl's lips set and a hard steely look made his blue eyes glint.

"As you say." Young Harcot studied the earl's face a moment before proceeding. "However, the new owner turned around and sold it at a considerable profit. The gentleman he sold it to fell onto difficult times and ran up a debt. He had no choice but to put up this choice piece of land as collateral with the Nottingham Bank. He was unable to pay his mortgage and the Bank ran a foreclosure sale. A gentleman, whose name you may know, picked up the parcel for the price of the foreclosure, oh, just about two years ago. He, however, has since passed away," he frowned over this, "leaving us with a somewhat awkward situation."

"And why is that?" However, the earl forestalled Harcot's answer, as a footman appeared with the coffee tray. The earl dismissed him and served Harcot his coffee. "I am sorry. Now, as you were saying? We have an awkward situation?"

"Indeed, my lord. The heir insists on knowing the identity of the interested party."

"And who was this man, may I ask?" the earl inquired thoughtfully, his long fingers forming a pyramid at his lips.

"Bartholomew. Sir Jasper Batholomew, as you may know was an elderly gentleman when he married. He left a young widow," Harcot hesitated, "Lady Anne." He found at this juncture that he was not able to meet the earl's very discerning eyes. He instead took a moment to study the unremarkable toes of his boots. His father was one of the earl's supporters, one of the few who had all the facts correctly in their place and had passed on his information to his son. The younger Harcot had on his first meeting with the earl discovered that he not only admired Cortland, but that he liked him as well. It was a source of embarrassment to be the bearer of this news. "I did not visit her myself. I thought it prudent to send a messenger with a short letter advising her only that we have a client interested in purchasing the land. We were careful to point out that these lands did not touch her own estates. She immediately sent a response with our messenger that she was not adverse to selling that which she felt she could not use, but that she would only do so upon being presented with the name of our client."

Harcot waited. He felt the earl's withdrawal. He

watched the earl's expression as memories of another time flitted through his mind. Harcot said regretfully, "A most unexpected development. I am sorry."

"She is, as she has always been . . ." Cortland began quietly. Then setting such thoughts aside, he smiled at his solicitor, "Thank you, Mr. Harcot, you have been quick and you have been thorough."

"Not at all." Harcot smiled ruefully. "The thing is, just what do we do now, my lord?"

"For the moment . . . nothing." The earl smiled softly. "It has been my experience that moving slowly and cautiously toward one's goals very often shows the way. We shall do so."

"Then, are you no longer interested in pursuing the matter at this time?"

"On the contrary." He stood up and extended his hand. "I mean to have that parcel of land, in my own good time." He smiled warmly at the younger man. "Harcot, I am pleased that you are representing me. Know that I appreciate the manner in which you handled my affair, and that I shall call upon you at your office in the near future."

Harcot felt supremely gratified. This was a young and successful man who had made his fortune in another country with very little help. He blushed with pleasure and, like a child, found he could not wait to report all of this to his exacting parent.

The earl stood and watched Harcot leave before going to the window, his hands clasped behind his back. He was much more bothered by this outcome than he had displayed to his solicitor. That Lady Anne should own the tract of land and waterway his brother had so carelessly gambled away was immensely irritating. There was no doubt Lady Anne would dangle it before his eyes and use it to trap him if she could. If she could? Therein lies the key, he thought as an idea began to form in his imagination.

He smiled then to himself, as he always did in the face of strong adversity. Lady Anne was a creature of whims, foibles and many weaknesses. Perhaps, just perhaps, before he disclosed himself to her, it would be beneficial to know *all* the vices she had collected along the way to her present situation. Indeed, Aunt Lucinda, he thought to himself, if ever I needed you, I need you now!

"Ah, Ned, deuced good to see you, old boy," ejaculated Oscar as Stendly opened the breakfast parlor door, stood aside and allowed him and Harry access. As Oscar smiled at Ned, he turned to give Harry a meaningful glare, for earlier that morning they had decided between them that Harry would be the one to take Ned aside and grill him about his late night larking. His job, happily enough, was to keep Sophy's attention in idle conversation.

Ned eyed Oscar quizzically. He liked these two friends of Sophy's. They had been around Egan Grange most of his life. They were often quite silly, but very genuine and he knew they sympathized with him in his desire to attend Harrow. In addition to these qualities, neither Harry nor Oscar ever seemed to notice the fact that he had an infirmity. They scarcely acknowledged his club foot. In times past they had even taught him to play cricket. They simply treated him as they would any lad, in fact, as they might if he were their own brother; he treated them much the same. "Hallo Oscar, have a muffin, they are wondrously good this morning and there is some of Cook's strawberry jam."

Instantly diverted, Oscar's hazel eyes lit up. "No, is there? Well, think I will." He paused on his way to the muffins and jam to drop a kiss on Sophy's cheek and say brightly, "Good morning, Soph, you look as lovely as the day."

Harry grimaced at him and Sophy laughed out loud, for very little got by her. She made a pouting face to tease the young man, "Why Harry, don't *you* think so?"

He rushed to assure her that he did indeed, that he thought her far more lovely than the day, and brought her delicate hands fervently to his lips as proof of his ardor.

Sophy giggled and told him not to be a noddy.

He eyed her reproachfully. "Sophia."

Sophy smiled at such antics and gently removed her hands from his very firm grip to rap his arm and advise him in soft amiable tones, "I am *so* very sorry Harry, but I fear I must chase you off this morning. I have never been so very inundated with tasks as I am today, and Ned was just about to finish eating his *last,*" she looked her brother's way, "muffin, so that *he* may give poor Mr. Grimms his full attention and cooperation this morning."

Ned sighed in answer to this. "Soph."

Oscar had buttered and jammed his muffin, and then quickly swallowed his first bite as he moved in to take up Sophy's elbow with his free hand. "Soph, a moment of your time, please?"

There was something compelling in the tone of Oscar's voice and Sophy turned a surprised look his way. "Well of course, Oscar."

"Thought you might like to know," he whispered as he drew her away from the center of the room to a cozy corner, "about this, er, Luddite situation."

Sophy's green eyes sparkled with interest. "Yes, yes I would."

In the meantime, Harry had drawn Ned aside and whispered, "Well, halfling, your rig is up. A thousand pities, I know, but there it is. You've been nabbled and Oscar and I don't mean to let this one go."

"Huh?"

"Oh, you mean to play off innocent airs, but they won't do, my lad. Saw you plain as pikestaff." This Harry knew was not quite true. They had seen someone carrying a lantern, but both he and Oscar had only guessed that it was Ned. However, Harry was now on a course. "It is time to call a halt to your bobberies."

Ned's mouth was open wide. He genuinely had no notion what Harry could be referring to. "My bobberies? Harry, what are you talking about?"

Harry shook his head. "Can't say I blame you. At your age, cooped up here alone, when anyone can see you should be with your peers at Harrow. However, it won't do, Ned."

"What won't do?"

Harry sighed for though he knew at Ned's age he would have been hard pressed to confess, he had hoped Ned would do so. That would have settled the matter in Harry's eyes. He gave it all he had, "We saw you last night you know."

"Last night?" Dawning lit. *"Oh!* Harry it was famous! What an adventure we had!"

"We?" Harry was surprised into asking.

"Yes. When Soph and I followed the fellow with the lantern—"

"Sophy and you? Sophy?" interrupted Harry, completely taken aback. "Never say Sophy was with you? Do

you mean to tell me that you and Sophy were skulking about the grounds in the dark?" Harry had been betrayed into nearly a shout which immediately drew Sophy and Oscar's full attention.

"Well, yes, but we were following someone—"

"Who were you following?" Harry demanded.

"If we knew that, we wouldn't have had to follow him." Ned shook his head over Harry's density in the matter.

Harry turned to Sophy. "Just what is going on here?"

"It is true," Sophy answered reasonably. "Something odd is going on and I am beginning to think it has something to do with this King Ludd and his Luddites that Oscar has been telling me about."

Fifteen

When Lucinda Morley had been eighteen and in her first season, she had managed to catch the man the *haute ton* had declared the marriage prize of the decade. He had been ten years her senior and though she had neither beauty nor a handsome dowry to recommend her, she caught his attention. To everyone's amazement and to many women's chagrin, the Duke of Bellevedere had fallen hopelessly, devotedly in love with Lucinda. Shortly afterward, he made her his duchess. For the next forty years, and until the time of his death, the Duke and Duchess of Bellevedere had been very nearly inseparable.

Lucinda had lost her parents before she was twenty and took into her care a sister some ten years younger. They were very close and when the time came, Lucinda was pleased to launch her young sister into the society she had quickly learned to rule. Lucinda liked the Earl of Cortland, and though he was a widower with son, she did not object when Cortland offered for her fair sister. A year later, childless herself, Lucinda had been ecstatic when presented with a nephew, Chase, Cortland's second son.

From the start, Lucinda had doted on her nephew and very nearly adopted him after her sister's untimely death. She was very sorely grieved when he had found himself, at only twenty years old, in a situation that caused him to leave for India.

Lucinda had been a distraught widow for two years, but with the return of her nephew, she made the decision to put off her blacks. She knew just what she was going to do. She would take her nephew, who had very fortuitously inherited the title, under her capable and far reaching social wings. She would see his reputation cleared and set him up as the next undisputed leader of the *haute ton*.

She had never been a beauty in the classical sense, but she had style at its best. Even at sixty-five she was considered one of London's leading hostesses. Her social prowess had been unquestioned for years. Thus, she had no doubt that this was a feat she could easily accomplish.

As her coach rumbled along the long winding drive, she smiled to herself, well pleased with the renovations her nephew had set into progress. Cortland Abbey and its Nabob Earl would certainly give her fuel for her campaign! Her driver pulled up the large coach to a halt in front of the Abbey's huge courtyard entrance. A lackey in Cortland livery rushed forward to open her door and offer her assistance, and the earl, having caught sight of her coach from his study window, was not far behind.

He felt light-hearted and happy as he rushed to greet her and a grin lit his handsome features. He inclined his head as he took up her gloved fingers. "Sixty-five, is it?" He shook his head. "Impossible, you dazzling creature, you."

It wasn't mere flattery. Lucinda was a tall, fashionable, most magnificent woman. She wore a rich brown velvet traveling ensemble that had been cut by a modiste of the first stare. Ivory lace at her throat and cuffs was perhaps ruffled to the point of flamboyance, yet suited her well.

A matching wide-brimmed hat was trimmed in the same lace, and a fine weaved net shaded her forehead of wispy white bangs. Her white soft waves were cut short and made a lovely frame for her ivory complexion. She laughed at his compliment and reached upwards to kiss his cheek. "Mountain! Even *I* must climb to my toes to reach you." She eyed him critically, "You look well, better in fact, than when last I saw you. Is it your fresh country air?"

She had been the first person he had visited when he arrived in London some months ago. His feelings upon returning to England had been mixed and he had not slept well during the voyage home. He smiled in agreement. "The air, the Abbey. Roland never loved this place, but like father I did, I do."

"Roland only loved the cut of the cards. How a gentleman of your father's cut ever spawned such a creature is more than I can fathom!"

The earl inclined his head, "I often wondered much the same, but never mind that now, Lucy. Come and see what we have done!"

Lady Anne Bartholomew, wearing a pretty morning gown of soft blue muslin, glided purposely toward her morning room. It was a quaint room that she had only recently re-papered and re-furnished in shades of blue and gold. However, this morning she was not thinking of decor. She had been losing sleep and all because of Chase Cortland!

She was not going to be discouraged by their slow beginning. After all, he was no doubt suffering some hurt pride on her account. She would have to first tend to that and put the blame on her family, on circumstances, on anything that would make him forget that part of their past.

In the meantime, something was troubling her. She went to her gold and white painted writing desk and her slender fingers rifled through a stack of opened, but unanswered mail. Just where was that letter from that Nottingham solicitor? There was something about it that rang a bell in her busy mind. She found first a note she had scribbled to the earl and then changed her mind about sending. She read it over again and sighed as she set it aside. In the past, all that would have been needed was her name to entice him to do for her. Now, all that was changed. It was frustrating to think that Chase was just outside her grasp. She was, she rightly believed, even more beautiful at nine-and-twenty than she had been at seventeen. Then, he had loved her to desperation. Now, he held back and kept her at bay. She must find a way of recapturing his affections, because she had decided she wanted Chase Cortland, or more importantly, his wealth and the power that came with such fabulous wealth!

She was certainly financially comfortable, but the competence her late husband had left her was not enough for her needs. There were so many things she wanted. Top on this list was London and its exciting Beau Monde! Bartholomew had taken her at her insistence for one season. His wealth was modest and though she had developed a fever to return, she wished to do so in style. She wanted to be able to afford the lavish establishment she wished to set up in London. She wanted to lead London's *ton!* That was her present dream and the earl with all his reputed wealth was the means.

With that goal in mind, she had gone to the Reddings'

soirée last night, thinking he might be there. She knew that he had been invited. Sadly, he had not been present. How was she to work her wiles on him if she could not get to him?

These thoughts ransacked her mind as she rifled through her stack of letters on her desk. Where was that blasted letter? Ah, here. From a Mr. Harcot, who did not identify his client. Why not? This question had tickled her curiosity during the night, and then she remembered something about this particular parcel of land. Bartholomew had said he had purchased a westerly tract of land that he could not presently use, but that he had paid very little for it. He had laughed to tell her that it was one more thing he had managed, indirectly, to steal from her old flame. At that time, she had not paid this any heed, for Bartholomew was forever jealous and saying odd things. Now, however, it was beginning to mean something. Her eyes narrowed as she put Harcot's letter up to scrutiny in the morning light and reread its contents. Well, well, here was Chase Cortland, renovating the Abbey, and suddenly someone wants to buy *this* particular tract of land. Odd.

Lady Anne looked at her reflection in the large, gold-framed mirror directly in front of her. Coincidence? She put up her chin and decided that she was every inch a beauty, but if her suspicions proved true, she had one more ace in the hole.

As Lady Anne's cunning mind whirled with plots and schemes, a lively discussion was in progress at Egan Grange. Harry with his finger wagging was directing a meaningful glare at his best friend. "Oscar shouldn't be worrying your head with Luddite talk."

"And why not? Does it not affect us all? Just what is going on? Why should you two, of all people, be attending secret meetings about these wretched, starving workers? And it was a secret meeting, wasn't it?" Sophy returned on a frown.

"Such meetings should not be a female's concern," snapped Harry again glaring at Oscar who eyed him in return.

"Don't be a noddy." Oscar pulled a face and added, "People are running about Egan Grange at night carrying lanterns doing who knows what, and you don't think Sophy should be told about the Luddite meeting? For pity's sake Harry, Soph and her brother were trotting hot foot in pursuit after the devil last night. She ain't your average female." Oscar was now shaking his head.

"Well," said Harry grudgingly, "I suppose when you put it that way." He sighed. "The sorry truth is that I wish we hadn't been a part of that meeting last evening. Don't want to lend that tallow-faced Branden countenance." Harry shook his head sadly. "If ever there was a vulgar make-bait of a man."

"Sophy the fellow was frothing at the mouth when he talked." Oscar visibly shuddered at the memory.

"The thing is, he seems to think these Luddites are planning to riot here in Nottingham." Harry frowned thoughtfully.

"He is a weasel of a man and should be held accountable for his crimes against the hard-working Englishmen in his employ!" retorted Sophy.

Oscar's brow went up. "Well, yes, that is true enough. But Sophy, when did you come across the twiddle-poop?"

Ned laughed out loud. "Yes, Oscar, that's what he is. We see him at church. He used to make mush-eyes at

Sophy but she gave him a proper set down. *I* wanted to kick him in the shins, but Soph wouldn't let me."

"Shame that," sympathized Oscar whose imagination came alive.

"May the devil take his eyes and feed them to the creatures of the underworld!" put in Harry with deep feeling.

Sophy eyed both Harry and Oscar with some amusement, but allowed this to pass unanswered, turning instead to address her wayward brother. "Which reminds me, young man, upstairs."

Ned got to his feet and moved toward the doorway, grumbling, but certainly complacent. He was clever enough to know his sister would presently brook no argument. At any rate, he had the projected afternoon adventure to look forward to. Thus, he was able to smile as he left for the schoolroom.

Sophy watched his retreating form before she returned her attention to the gentlemen at hand to say, "So then, tell me. Weasel Branden called a meeting and everyone jumped to his tune?" Her brow was up and there was the glint of disgust in her green eyes.

"That isn't why *we* went, Soph." Harry immediately went on the defensive. "We were there to see what was toward. Our sympathies, and we are not alone, are with the Luddites." He eyed Sophy reproachfully. "Thought *you* would know that."

She touched his arm, "I do. So then, just what did you discover? What does the weasel mean to do?"

"Branden is a wealthy man, Soph," Oscar was shaking his head. "Has called in a Bow Street Runner already to search out the Luddites and discover who their King Ludd might be. Means to call in an army if he has to in order to defend his mill."

"Bow Street Runners? An army to defend his mill? Against what, may I ask?" requested Miles Egan within the library doorway.

"Papa," said Sophy happily as she went to him. "I thought you were still at your desk with your writing. Here let me pour you some coffee. I think it is still quite hot."

"No, no coffee, child." He touched her cheek and moved towards the sofa, turning to Harry to ask, "Well then, young man, why does Branden think he needs a Bow Street Runner?" He patted a place on the sofa for his daughter to sit beside him.

Filled with a sense of importance, Harry quickly and portentously apprised Sophy's father of the facts he had at hand, summing it up with, "It is hard to say just where all this is going."

"Hmmm. There is to be a bill put before the House of Lords asking for the death penalty for Luddites caught smashing frames and looms. You, I don't think, are acquainted with Lord Byron, but I had the good fortune of meeting and spending some days with him last summer at a mutual friend's house." He smiled at his daughter, "You know them, darling, the Hobkins?"

Sophy nodded. "Oh, yes, I remember. Ned and I were at Aunt Gussie's. I thought it was terribly unfair of you to meet Byron without me." she pouted at her father and he pinched her nose.

"Indeed, you are quite right. At any rate, Lord Byron's estate, Newstead Abbey, is not far from Nottingham." He reached over to the dark oak coffee table and picked up the Nottingham *Chronicle*. "Here, allow me to read an excerpt of Byron's recent and very passionate speech on the subject." He perused the article a moment before reading aloud, "Suppose it passed. Suppose one of these men, as I have seen them, meager with famine, sullen with despair, careless of a life which your lordships are about to value at something less than the price of a stocking frame—suppose this man (and there are a thousand such) were dragged into court and tried for this new offense by this new law, still there are two things wanting to convict and condemn him; and these are, in my opinion, twelve butchers for a jury, and a Jeffreys for a judge . . ."

"Zounds!" ejaculated Oscar. "Well put, well put, indeed."

"Lord Byron, eh?" Harry was frowning. "Thought he was only a poet."

Miles Egan's brows snapped together. *"Only* a poet?"

Sophy came quickly to Harry's rescue. "Yes, a poet and obviously an Englishman with a sense of duty and a great deal of heart." She shook her head. "But, that still leaves us with men like Branden."

"We have nought to fear in Nottingham," said her father. "I don't expect the Luddites in our region to riot, even against the evil of a Branden."

"And why not?" Oscar asked doubtfully. "They have cause and they have that fellow they call King Ludd. No doubt he would like to see some action take place to further his cause."

"Branden thinks this King Ludd might even be a member of the gentry," said Harry thoughtfully.

"Indeed? Whatever makes him think so?" Miles Egan looked surprised. "It is most unlikely. It has been my observation that our class, with the exception of a few individuals, would much rather solve such ugly problems with conversation than with action."

"Mayhap, sir, but Branden says he thinks he has proof and that is why he has called in the runner."

"Proof? What kind of proof?" Sophy asked curiously.

Harry shook his head. "We haven't a clue, but, mark me these Bow Street Runners are the very devil to deal with."

"It is a sorry state of affairs when a man of Branden's stamp leads the flock," said Miles Egan sadly.

Sixteen

The earl had arrived a few moments before the prescribed hour and tethered his big black neatly out of the way. A quick glance down the stretch of field for sight of Sophy and her brother gave him an odd sensation of anticipation. However, they were not within view, and he quickly turned toward the edge of the thicket and began scouting for any discernible tracks left from the night before.

They were not difficult to find. However, careful scrutiny made him believe the tracks he found were their own. He followed these telltale signs for some distance and then stopped to glance thoughtfully around for something more. He found it at a patch of mud near the edge of the stream that criss-crossed into inlets and rivulets on its winding journey through Sherwood Forest. It was in this patch of hardened mud that he found something meaningful. He bent to his knees to inspect one very clear boot print that definitely did not belong to Sophy, Ned or himself.

"You've found something!" Ned declared in a fever pitch, as he scrambled forward from off in the distance. Sophy was right behind him, putting a warning finger to her pretty lips. "Hush, Neddy."

"Oh, I think we are quite alone this afternoon," the earl

said softly as he turned round to greet them. His blue eyes lit with sure appreciation as he found Sophy walking toward him. It suddenly occurred to him that he had never seen such a vibrant elfin beauty in his entire thirty-two years. Openly, and with a purposeful flourish he looked Sophy over. His blue twinkling eyes were very bright as they moved from her head to her toes and then to her warm green eyes. He made no attempt to hide his scrutiny from her, and had he been wearing a hat, he would have tipped it to her.

Sophia was all too aware that her form of dress was completely unconventional and that had she not been her own mistress at Egan, she would not have been allowed to leave the house dressed as she was. She blushed a little and her lashes shaded her eyes as she thought of the picture she presented, dressed in an old, waist length, tight fitting and oddly enough, alluring wool riding coat. No skirt covered her lower body, but tight-fitting britches displayed to advantage her slim curvaceous hips and long slender legs. Her flame colored hair was tied at the top of her head with a brown ribbon and fell in pretty profusion round her piquant face. Thick curls of red hair covered her forehead and more of the same twirled round her ears.

It was obvious he found her attractive, as he said on a note of amusement, "The latest in country attire, I take it?" He cocked his thick expressive brow at her.

She smiled naughtily and said, "Well, my lord, you would not expect me to ruin yet another gown, would you?"

"No, I would not. The thing is," he flicked her nose, "I wouldn't expect you to be out here scrambling about, either." He chuckled. "At least, it has been my experience that gently bred maids generally have better things to do. Getting dirty is not one of those things. So, there you are, what do I know?"

She laughed. "Now, what have you found?"

During this time, Ned had been inspecting the mud and turned a beaming face to her. "A boot print, Soph. But what good that does, I don't know, for it seems to stop here."

"Not so, Neddy," said the earl. "If you cast a glance across this tiny stream you will see that the edge," he held Ned's shoulder and pointed, "there, has been pushed downward by someone landing heavily."

"By Jove, yes, my lord," Ned exclaimed excitedly. "Come on, then!"

Sophy eyed the width of the narrow stream with some misgiving. "Come on? You mean jump it?"

"If you want an adventure . . ." The earl grinned wickedly.

"Hold on then, I'll go get my mare. That is how I jump streams," bantered Sophy.

Ignoring her remark, the earl called to Ned, "Go on, lad, I'll look after your sister."

Ned was very happy to comply with this, and both the earl and Sophy watched the boy maneuver the sedately flowing water's width in spite of his club foot.

Sophy applauded him. "Well done, Neddy. Now, if only *I* can manage it."

"You'll do fine," encouraged the earl. "I'll help you."

"Unless you mean to jump it for me, I don't see how you can help me," Sophy answered him quizzically.

Without speaking another word, the earl turned around and easily leaped across the stream which was beginning to look wider and wider to Sophia. He turned, stepped down into its **muddy** rooty lower **bank and** reached for her. "Come along then, I'm here to catch you."

She braced herself and with a little yelp made the jump. She reached the bank's edge on the other side and was about to laugh with pleasure when she felt the heels of her shoes slipping backward into the mud. "Oh!"

Just as she thought she was going for a swim, she felt the earl's arm gently encompass her and soon he was scooping her up to safety. They stood together for a moment before Sophy giggled and remarked, "I thought for certain I was about to become very wet." She made no effort to leave the comfort of his enveloping embrace and instead made a strategic mistake; she looked up into his glittering blue eyes. Her lips parted and a sense of fairy-tale quality took over the moment. She tried to find level ground for though she felt breathless with excitement, she knew she had to return to reality. Oh, but he was handsome, so very handsome! "Thank you. You are very, er, athletic," she managed to utter and felt a fool.

The earl met her look and felt mesmerized by her lush green eyes. There was a glow on her cheeks, and the smile on her lips was genuine, beautiful and most captivating. There was certainly no denying that he felt a sure stirring of desire. He immediately, silently cursed himself for acting like a schoolboy, and frowned as he attempted to shake off such traitorous sensations. "You are very welcome," he answered, his blue eyes glittering still, his voice soft and sweetly husky in spite of his self-reproach.

Sophy blushed and looked round in an attempt to get control of her wayward emotions. The earl took the moment to find himself and looked to see what Neddy was doing.

Neddy, apparently unconcerned with these proceedings,

continued his investigating, wandering further into the woods as broken low branches and crushed new spring buds pointed the way. He looked round and frowned to himself for his trail had led him closer to Cortland. There, in a stretch of soft earth he found another boot print and set up a shout.

The earl with Sophy close behind hurriedly jogged to him. The earl looked around as he bent down to inspect the print.

"Hmmm, it is the same. See this odd marking here at the heel? What doesn't fit is the fact that we have now moved into Cortland Woods."

Sophy leaned across him as she first looked at the print and then surveyed their surroundings. "Are you sure?"

"Aye, I am sure," said the earl thoughtfully, almost absently for his mind was already suggesting logical solutions to this oddity.

"It's the first thing I noticed, too, my lord," agreed Neddy who had a finger on his nose. "The thing is, this is where he put out his light, I'm sure of it. And if it is, well, he had a long way to go to walk to Sherwood in the dark, don't you think?"

"Yes, Neddy, I do," the earl grinned at him. "Very clever, lad. Think how brilliant you will be one day after you have consistently applied yourself to your studies?"

Neddy smiled sheepishly. "Yes, well I *would* apply myself if my father would see reason and allow me to attend Harrow."

Sophy sighed and walked off a few feet, looking around intently. "I do not see any signs that he went any further, do you?" She was still glancing round as she spoke.

The earl's countenance was troubled as he glanced around. Something just did not fit. He couldn't come up with a single answer to the obvious questions. There was something more to all of this than he had first thought, but what? "Right then. Where was our late night stroller headed, for what purpose and just who was he?" He spoke out loud, but, did not really expect a reply.

"A Bow Street Runner," answered Sophy ominously, "hired, no doubt, by Branden."

"A *runner?*" The earl was surprised and regarding Sophy with some respect. "Now what makes you say that? I do in fact think you are on the mark, for I rather thought the little chap I saw the other night at one of Nottingham's taverns was a runner. But who is Branden and why would he hire one?"

"A runner? *A Bow Street Runner?*" interjected Ned with great enthusiasm. "This is getting better every minute and makes me deuced glad I'm *not* at Harrow just now!"

Sophy and the earl laughed at this and then Sophy quickly explained about Oscar and Harry's conversation with her earlier that morning concerning the Luddites and Branden Mills.

"Harry and Oscar? The two fellows hovering over you at the ball?" asked the earl as he looked around and appeared only mildly interested in her response.

"Yes, they seem to think that there might be a problem with this King Ludd and his followers."

"And you? What do you think?" The earl was looking at her now.

Sophy shook her head. "I think our government should pay some heed to our working class."

The earl became thoughtful and finally said, "Come on, it will soon be getting dark." He started to lead them out of the woods.

"Oh yes, and your horse. I hope he will still be where

you left him," Sophy said in some concern. "My mare would have escaped her ties and wandered off by now," she added ruefully.

"He has been with me long enough to know his job. Besides, I don't imagine that with a field full of long grass, if he forgets himself and does go off he will wander too far."

Ned started back the way they had come, but Sophy put up a stern objection. "Oh no, I am *not* jumping that stream again."

The earl laughed and said he knew an easier route. He took her arm. Both were all too conscious of the touch, and to ease the moment, Sophy smiled and hurried along.

Seventeen

Lucinda glided toward the earl as he walked into the huge marbled central hall and exclaimed, "Ah, there you are! Well, I was beginning to think you were going to be wicked and run off."

The earl laughed and took her hand to his lips. "Run off? Now, why would I do that?"

"So, you *have* forgotten about tonight!" accused his aunt with a click of her tongue.

"Tonight?" Then as memory intruded, he pulled a comical face much like a young boy, and released an oath, "Blast, tonight." In a moment of weakness he had allowed her to wheedle a promise to escort her to a rout being given by an old friend of hers.

Her hands went to her hips. "Chase Cortland, never say you mean to renege?"

He recalled his promise with a heavy sigh. "No, no, of course not."

She patted his arm soothingly. "There, there dear. You are thinking it will be dull sport, but Hester gives the very best affairs. That is why I rushed here yesterday. I thought it would be pleasant for us to attend this particular gathering together. You will like Hester Saltash and her very intriguing set. She surrounds herself with a lively crew, writers, poets, and she is very political. Robert Owen and

Francis Place will be there, which is typical of Hester. Those two have very humble beginnings, though their work is very prominent. They will interest you, I know, as will Cobbett."

"I am not familiar with Owens or Place, but Cobbett is a devil of a fellow. He uses his *Political Register* to ridicule nearly everyone, sometimes without cause and to no purpose."

"That may be, but make no mistake, these sorts of characters are very entertaining. Imagine, he lived for some years in America, in a place called Long Island. I think you will enjoy the evening immensely. Besides, Hester adores her Nottingham gentry and never fails to invite all the county. She is a most unusual hostess. You will have a nice opportunity to meet your neighbors."

"Sly puss. That is what this is all about, isn't it?" He was smiling ruefully and wondering if Sophy would be there. She had not mentioned the rout.

They had moved down the long hall toward the library, but Woodly, at their back, was clearing his throat to catch the earl's attention. Cortland turned and Woodly inclined his head as he presented a silver salver. "This just arrived for you, my lord."

The earl's brow went up as he took the ivory envelope and received an impression of a familiar scent. He nodded to Woodly and took his aunt into the library. Lucinda attempted to make herself comfortable on an old, ornately carved wooden chair and grumbled loudly that her nephew needed some new furniture.

He chuckled as he lit a branch of candles at his desk after which he took up his letter opener. He then held up the short note paper to read:

Darling,

I have been made to recall that I own a tract of land that once belonged to your family.

Perhaps you are interested in owning it again?

Come tomorrow afternoon, and we shall discuss the matter at leisure.

Your loving,
Anne

"Damn her soul!" the earl hissed as he lost control of his temper.

"What, Chase? What is wrong?" Lucinda rose and went to him.

"Lady Anne. That is what is wrong. Lady Anne."

Miles Egan was pleased enough to escort his daughter to the Saltash rout. A great many of his literary friends were sure to be there, which would afford him a pleasant evening. Sophy smiled to see her father form a lively group with his friends and left Harry and Oscar, who had made the twenty-minute drive with them in Mr. Egan's coach, to their own devices as she moved to join two of her friends who were frantically waving for her attention.

Nathan Walker saw her as soon as he entered the room. She stood with two other young ladies, and all three were giggling with pleasure. He surveyed her with approval. She wore an ivory satin gown, invitingly trimmed at the heart shaped neck with ivory lace. The lace hung elegantly over her sleeveless shoulders, made a wide waistband, and ornamented the hem of the gown's narrow skirt. The dress hugged her tall, lithe figure in alluring lines. Her thick, flame colored tresses were gathered at the top of her head with an ivory ribbon and were pinned in cascading curls around her well shaped head. Pearls adorned her ears and neck in classic style. Nathan complimented himself on his choice of bride. He moved in her direction. Just at that moment, both Harry and Oscar looked round from their circle of friends to see Nathan moving toward Sophy.

"See," said Harry pulling a face. "Knew it. Told you the other day this was going to happen. Was bound to. Sophy isn't a hoyden schoolgirl anymore, is she? He went to visit her, saw that she was a diamond, then decided to make a push to have her!"

"But will Soph have him?" returned Oscar superiorly.

"Noddy! Soph was all cow's eyes for him years ago," snapped Harry

"Don't set the least store by that. After all, Harry, that was years ago, she was a child. As a matter of fact, so were we." He gave this some thought. "Played one or two nasty boys' pranks on her as well. The wonder is she never minded." Oscar regarded Harry gravely, "The thing is, I don't think Soph will have you either."

"Don't you, my man?" Harry nearly spluttered. "Then who will she have? *You?*"

Oscar put up his chin, "As well as *you.*"

While their altercation dived into absurdity, Nathan Walker was indeed making every effort to court Sophy's attention. He bent over her hand to say quietly, "Sophy, you are the prettiest woman here."

Sophy blushed, but not because she was flattered. He had excluded her friends, and she quickly looked their way to introduce them. Walker was a gentleman and paid proper attention to this introduction. His voice when he spoke to the girls was soft and he exchanged amenities with them in a light and pleasant fashion. She could find no fault, and yet there was something in his eyes that betrayed him. He was bored and impatient with them.

It was certainly true that her friends were a bit missish, and giggling, but they were genuinely excited and just a bit shy of him. Sophy thought they were perhaps intimidated by his air of sophistication. They knew their own social graces were not as polished as his, but they were her dear, adorable friends and she could see that Walker found them obviously silly. However, she was happy to see that they at least did not appear to notice the cold expression in Nathan Walker's eyes or his eagerness to quit their company. They continued to babble sweetly as Nathan took her bare arm to whisper, "May I steal you away for a little while?"

There was still the memory of her youth and her infatuation with Nathan Walker. She had not realized then that he was such a self-centered fellow. She had just never seen that side of him before. No doubt he had only tolerated her in those days because it had been flattering to his ego. But she was not given time to contemplate this observation as her attention was suddenly captivated by the arrival of a most distinguished man walking into the all too crowded room.

The earl's heart had been beating wildly as they entered Hester Saltash's huge ballroom. It was when he saw Sophy that he knew at once, it had been beating in anticipation of this moment. He had been hoping to find her this evening. Deuce fly away with this absurdity. He had to get control of himself!

His aunt drew him with her to meet Hester Saltash, and it was a long time he felt before he was able to break away and move across the room.

Hester Saltash was Lucinda's age, however, unlike her

friend, she was a diminutive woman who overate and over-dressed. She watched the earl as he purposely made his way across the crowded room and leaned to her friend to say boldly, "I like him. He'll do. Has backbone and bottom."

Lucinda smiled. "Yes and more, Hessie, he has such heart."

"Indeed, saw that in his eyes. Eyes always tell a story." Then she straightened to say, "Well, well." This succinct remark was accompanied by a knowing smile and a smug grunt.

Lucinda eyed her little round friend with impatience. Hester was always doing things like that. She would rarely finish a sentence, and, thus, kept you on her line. It was most irritating. "Well, well? *Faith,* don't stop there, Hessie!"

"Look for yourself," said her friend pugnaciously. The earl had reached Sophy and Nathan Walker at that moment and was bowing low over Sophy's lace gloved fingers. When he brought his blue eyes up to find her face, there was a soft smile on his lips, drawing one from hers.

Lucinda could see that here was a local diamond and asked at once, "Who is she?"

"Sophia Egan. Odd, I wouldn't have thought her in his style." Hester shrugged.

Lucinda took umbrage. "And what, pray, do you imagine is in his style?"

"Oh, come down from the boughs. I only meant that, well, he is two-and-thirty, isn't he? She is only a babe, not yet twenty. He is a sophisticated traveler and Sophia is a country girl. A darling beauty to be sure, but she lacks airs. So different than Anne was . . . is."

Lucinda's fingers were snapping in the air. "That to

age. My own dear Bellevedere was so much older than I. As to Anne, *she* was never in his style. He didn't really know her. You called Miss Egan a darling. Does that mean you like her?"

"Well, of course I do. That is just it. Wouldn't want to see her get hurt. She has never met a man of his stamp."

"What makes you think that my nephew would hurt her?" Lucinda's chin was up and there was a militant sparkle in her eyes.

"Lucy, Lucy. I am not saying he would intend to hurt her, but well, there you are," Hester was sighing and indicating with her chin and eyes, "Look for yourself!"

Lucinda was left to contemplate this as she watched her nephew lead Sophia Egan out of the room!

Eighteen

Nathan Walker was inwardly in a rage. He wasn't often given to fits of temper, but knew well how to conceal them. A man in his position, living on the edge of the Beau Monde's hedonistic world, would not survive otherwise. He could see that the earl, with a deft skill, had managed the situation to his advantage. It was Sophy's fault for saying how hot and stuffy the overcrowded room had become. The room was inundated with people and she was right, it *was* hot, but this had given the earl his opportunity. Nathan shook his head, for it had been his own fault for acting the gentleman and offering to fetch her a cool drink. However, it had been a devious maneuver of the earl's, to whisk her away, saying that what she should have was some fresh air. Damnation! Well, he would not be outdone by rank and fortune. For as long as he could remember, Sophy had always seemed to think him a knight in shining armor. He was very certain she still felt that way. What he would quickly do was to find a footman to fetch him a glass of fresh, cool negus and take it right out to her.

Even as he went about this he had to admit to himself that he was surprised at Cortland. What was the earl about? Playing fast and loose with an innocent girl who was not quite up to snuff. Anyone could see that was all Sophia really was. He had rather liked Cortland and had thought better of him. At that moment he looked round and discovered a new arrival; Lady Anne.

She looked absolutely stunning. She moved with grace and a sure style. Her white-gold hair was piled high and fastened with blue silk roses to match her soft and clinging gown of blue silk and silvery lace. However, though he found her attractive, she had caught his attention because he had recognized her as the woman who had audaciously and very improperly broken with social protocol, arriving at the Abbey to visit the earl alone. A certain amount of curiosity had inspired him to draw the earl into conversation and to casually remark on her beauty. The earl had ruefully agreed and mentioned that they had known one another a long time ago. Well, she looked to be more in his style than Sophia. Perhaps, this little piece of information might prove useful. Indeed, there was even the chance that he could play it as a trump card this very evening.

Lady Anne had walked in on the arm of one of her many local admirers. She looked round the room and, though she did not see the earl, she did see Lucinda, Duchess of Bellevedere, and one fine light brow went up with interest. She lost no time in going to Lucinda to exclaim in her society voice, "Darling, you here in Nottingham? Whatever brings you here at this time of year?"

Lucinda had witnessed Lady Anne's dashing entrance and then her mad rush to reach her. She knew precisely what Anne's motive was. "Anne, how nice. You are looking as lovely as ever."

"Am I?" cooed Anne. "As you are, dearest." Then because Anne had ever been impatient to have whatever struck her fancy, she found a way of getting to the point. "Are you staying with Hester?"

Very good, thought Lucinda, very neat. "No, I am staying with Chase."

"Really? How lovely for you both." She looked round. "No doubt he escorted you here tonight? I shall go and find him as there is something of a business nature that I must discuss with him."

"Yes, of course, Anne. I understand," said Lucinda leaving no doubt as to her meaning. She wanted Lady Anne to know that she was fully aware of her game.

Lady Anne had the knack of allowing meaningful statements to roll off unheeded. She smiled brightly and moved off to do a leisurely tour of the room.

The garden was a lovely square landscape of stone. Evergreens lined different avenues as did various flowering trees and shrubs. Daffodils filled flower beds and there was a fresh spring scent in the cool night breeze. The earl led Sophy off the flagstone terrace and down one of the paths laid out in red brick. He was chuckling and she was laughing sweetly as he recounted one of his indiscretions during his early months in India.

As Sophy's giggles subsided she sighed. "I should dearly like to travel to India and to America and oh, everywhere. I think I have the heart of a gypsy."

"And the soul of an angel," the earl said softly.

She looked up at him and all at once he couldn't stop himself. He had her tucked into his arms and was bending to gently drop a kiss on her cherry lips. He drew back as though singed by a hot flame and found her warm green eyes welcoming him. All control was gone as he tightened his embrace and found her mouth once more!

There was a rush of feeling as his desire seemed to blend with something he could not, would not name. Conscience intruded and he heard a voice clicking off words. Cad, scoundrel, how can you take advantage of such an angel? Stop! She is an innocent girl! He yanked himself away, almost thrusting her from him. "Forgive me . . ."

There wasn't time for her to think or to respond as they heard voices at their backs. They sprang guiltily away and turned round to find Nathan Walker, a glass of negus in one hand, and Lady Anne at the other, as he led her toward them.

"Oh, here you are. I thought I saw you go out for air," said Nathan amiably as he presented Sophy with the negus. She thanked him, but there was nothing she wanted less, particularly as she watched Lady Anne slip her arm through the earl's and kiss his cheek. Sophy flushed with sudden irritation. She knew Lady Anne only by sight, for they usually traveled in different circles. However, she could see that the earl seemed to know her very well.

Nathan took Sophy's elbow and said for her ears alone, "Come, Sophia. Lady Anne and the earl have a great deal to talk about." Before she could speak, he turned to incline his head towards Lady Anne and smile at the earl. "I will return Miss Egan to the ballroom."

"We will go with you. The night air is getting cooler by the minute," the earl interjected as he moved toward them, and there was a sure glint of anger in his blue eyes.

"My lord, a moment of your time," whispered Anne softly as she held his upper arm and delayed him. The earl turned to glance at her thoughtfully. This was not the time to insult her. Anne could be vindictive. She would hold onto his land just for spite.

Sophy could not help but notice that the earl turned to give the blond beauty his full attention. She felt herself cringe inwardly. He was of course a seasoned rake, totally capable of stealing her kisses and then moving on to another conquest. She bolstered herself and turned sharply to smile a touch too brightly at Nathan. She heard herself chattering nonsense, but couldn't seem to stop the flow. All she wanted to do was get away and leave the sight of a notorious widow and the man she, Sophy, had just allowed to kiss her lips. Her innate honesty had already rejected the notion that the earl had stolen a kiss. Indeed, she had given it freely.

"Darling," purred Lady Anne as her finger stroked the earl's lean cheek.

He felt his hairs stand on end. However, this was not the time to reject her advances. He would play her game and see what she had in her scheming little mind. His father would have been heartsick had he watched his eldest son gamble away Cortland land. Because of his father's memory he was nearly obsessed with regaining that tract of land. "Yes, pretty girl?" He smiled easily, but a more discerning individual would have noted the cold set of his sensuous lips. Nor did the lady observe that his smile did not reach his deep blue eyes. "Did you not receive the letter I sent over to you today, Chase?" Her lashes coyly stroked her eyes.

"I did and I was going to send you a note and invite you to call. Lucinda is staying with me, so we now have proper chaperonage," he grinned flirtatiously.

"Ah, but *now* we are old enough to ignore a propriety or two," offered the lady huskily.

"Perhaps your reputation can afford to do so, mine, however, can not. Come tomorrow and we will have privacy enough when we take a tour of the grounds." There was a warm sound to his words and he could see they had their affect on her. As she put her arms round his waist, he took strong hold of her wrists and moved a step backward, smiling as he whispered, "Come Anne. With *our* history, we don't want to give the gossipmongers any more meat to chew."

"I hope you did not mind the interruption?" Nathan Walker asked Sophy gently as they re-entered the ballroom.

"No, of course not." She smiled and then managed to inquire casually, "I am not really acquainted with Lady Anne, but she is certainly a very beautiful woman."

"Indeed and having come to know the earl, I rather think they are well suited for one another." Nathan Walker lowered his voice at this point. "I have a notion she and the earl are, in fact, more than friends. Seems to me there just might be a romance brewing between them." There, he admired his handiwork. Truth to tell he rather thought his words were not so very far from the facts.

"Really?" Sophy's heart was beating wildly but she contrived to appear unconcerned. "What makes you say so?"

"Lady Anne came out to the Abbey just a few days ago," he dropped his voice meaningfully to add, *"alone."*

Sophy felt a sharp pain shoot through her. She put up her chin bravely and said quietly, "No doubt, as you say, they are well suited."

Nineteen

Sophy looked into her brother's room with an impatient click of her tongue. How could he have run off again? Mr. Grimms had every right to be disgusted with Ned's thoughtless behavior. She had no doubt whatsoever that Mr. Grimms was on the verge of leaving them. As she expected, Ned's room was empty. She had known that he would not be there, of course, but she had wanted to give him the benefit of the doubt. Sophy was in sad straits, and this latest mischief easily fired her temper. With a militant sparkle in her dark green eyes, she began an earnest search for Ned in the house during which she told herself that when she found him, she would wring his young neck!

Downstairs she came upon Stendly, who made a quick turnabout in an attempt to avoid his young mistress. Sophy's brow went up and she called him to a halt in the long corridor. There was the light of unmistakable suspicion on her face and in her voice. "Stendly?"

"Yes, miss?"

"Right then, shall we cut to the chase, my dear fellow?"

Resigned, the favored retainer sighed, "Yes, miss. Mr. Ned went out early this morning and promised me he would return before you started looking for him."

"I see. Thank you, Stendly." Sophy's mood was already

black and though normally this would have brought a rueful smile to her face, it lacked the power to do so at that
moment. Sophia Egan grimaced as she reached for the
shawl she kept on a hook near the back door. She wrapped
it round her shoulders and, with a flounce of her pretty
blue muslin gown, made her way outdoors.

Sophy had not slept well. Her mind had not allowed
her to rest as it kept reliving the events of the evening.
How excited she had been when she had discovered the
earl at the rout. Her mind's eye could see him still—he
was so very handsome, and stood out amongst the crowd.
How thrilled she had been to be singled out by him. She
held herself now, as she recalled how her body had trem-
bled when she had walked beside him in the courtyard
garden. She didn't know how it happened, but then, all at
once she was in his arms. His kiss had made everything
in the world seem so wonderful and perfect. Then just as
suddenly, that same kiss had plunged her into deep confusion!

Nathan Walker had returned her to the overcrowded
ballroom. There, though she had found herself surrounded
with her friends and ardent admirers, she could not help
looking for the earl's return. It seemed a long time before
he re-entered the ballroom and, when he did, she found
the sight of Lady Anne on his arm made her feel nearly
sick with jealousy. Jealousy? It was a terrible disease and
she wanted none of it. She must get control of herself!

Then, if all that had not been enough to throw her off
balance, she became aware of a sure and sudden tenseness
that scurried through the room as heads had turned to
watch Cortland and Lady Anne arm in arm. No doubt,
Nathan was right, and the earl meant to court the notorious
widow. The notion swung Sophy's habitual good humor

into quiet depression. To alleviate her bleak mood, she forced herself into a ritual of merriment. She teased Oscar and Harry, she danced with nearly everyone, she frolicked playfully with her friends and totally ignored the earl's presence. She had been completely miserable.

The sound of twigs being crushed into dewy wet leaves brought her attention to the woods and she spied Ned coming toward her through the thicket. "Ned!" she said in tones meant to convey her displeasure.

"Soph! I am glad you are here. There is something I have to show you," he responded innocently as he reached for her hand.

"Is there, really, young man?" Sophy could not help but smile as he approached. She had never been able to resist the open affection he always displayed toward her, and she bent to receive the kiss on the cheek he was obviously offering. "Even so, Ned, you must know you are in my black books this morning?"

He hung his head. "I am sorry Soph, thought I'd be back before you came down to breakfast."

"Did you? Then why for pity's sake were you not? Don't you realize poor Mr. Grimms is at his wit's end?" Soph's hands were tapping her trim hips.

"I didn't mean to be late, though in truth, Soph, I wish he *would* leave," Ned answered wistfully. "I'm too old for a tutor. Makes me feel a fool."

Sophy's sympathy was immediately aroused and she relented with a sigh, "Yes, Neddy, I know. Never mind then, perhaps Mr. Grimms will move on and Papa will have no choice then. He would have to enlist you at Harrow."

Ned's eyes lit with sudden desperation. "Gammon! He

would just send for another tutor, that's what he has always done."

Sophy put her arm around him. "Never mind that now. Somehow we shall find a way to reach Papa soon. What have you to show me?"

"You recall yesterday when we were searching after those footprints with the earl? They just stopped which didn't make any sense. I wanted to go have a look and see if we missed a spot."

"Oh, Neddy, I don't think so. We combed the area—" started his sister doubtfully.

"Yes, but only on the north side. Think about it Sophy, if he crossed the stream where it's narrow, just as we did—"

His sister cut him off. "Yes, but Ned, that just doesn't fadge." She was frowning thoughtfully. "Or does it?"

"Just so. It would if you wanted to throw off the scent," retorted Ned. "And, Soph, that's what he did!" He ended triumphantly.

"You found something? On your own, Neddy? *Faith!*" She touched his nose. "Clever lad, show me!"

They made their way through the woods to the spot where they had jumped across the other day. Here Sophy sighed an objection, but her young brother reassured her merrily. "No, Soph you don't have to jump. He came back over the stream further down where it is not as wide as it is here." He took her hand and led her slowly along to a part of the stream where in fact only a trickle of rushing water swept a rocky bed. There he bent to point a finger, "See here." Then Ned got to his feet and moved further up a rise to point to yet another undisturbed heel print. "And here." He turned to beam brightly at her. "What do you think?"

Sophy's fine brows were drawn together as she studied

the sudden rise of ground. She had never really noticed this particular hill. Just where had their night visitor vanished to when he extinguished his lantern? Had their mysterious trespasser climbed over this considerable hill without benefit of light?

There was no time for further contemplation of this problem as a sharp sound startled them both. They spun round and saw a short, husky fellow in a dark blue coat and peaked cap turn and rush off into the woods.

Sister and brother regarded one another for a moment, then without a word gave chase!

It was early morn and the earl was about to take his leave of his aunt, as they stood together in front of the huge fireplace in the Prior's Parlor. Lucy was thoughtfully studying the restored tapestry which hung above the dark oak mantle, but clicked her tongue to stall the earl's departure, "Very nice, indeed, but," she hesitated a moment before touching her nephew and said, "darling, don't you think," she glanced round the nearly barren room and pulled a face, "that you need a woman's fine touch?" She stood back and watched for his reaction as her hazel eyes twinkled.

"Yours?" he smiled at her. "Be my guest, do what you will."

She frowned. "No, no. It would be nice if you had a bride to do that for you." She had given it her best shot.

"Ah, not planning on playing at matchmaker while you are here, dearest, are you?" he retorted with an affectionate smile. He took her elbow to lead her out.

"Not I? At least, I don't see the need. You manage the

game quite well on your own," she flung back at him merrily.

His expressive brow went up. "Now, just what is that remark supposed to mean?"

She laughed. "Cat and mouse is such a pleasant pastime when one is the cat."

"Lucinda!" he warned, "If you know what is good for you, best of my relations . . ."

"Yes, yes love, I am only teasing after all. I will tell you one thing though. Last evening, there was an enchantingly lively redhead. Let me see, what did Hester say her name was?" She managed not to look directly at him, yet she could see his face.

"Sophia Egan?" he supplied, though his bantering tones had hardened and his eyes took on a cold aloofness.

"Ah, yes such a vivacious beauty. I don't think even Lady Anne in her heyday compared to her." It was bait of a sort.

It took. "Lady Anne compare to Soph—Miss Egan? She isn't fit to walk the same earth!"

"Ah" returned Lucinda thoughtfully, "I thought not." She had expected a response along this line, however it had been flung back at her with a depth of feeling that had caught even the knowing Lucinda off guard. She touched his arm gently. "Did Anne hurt you so very badly, Chase?"

"She hurt the boy." He smiled. "Not the man, and the boy is gone."

"Is he, darling?" Lucinda touched his arm affectionately. "I wonder?"

"Soph! This way," called Ned as he stopped to catch his breath and scan the woods for the man they had been chasing. They had lost sight of him in the thicket, but Ned caught the flash of his dark blue coat as he weaved through the woods.

"Hurry, I am with you." His sister was behind him in a split second. She had taken another path a few moments before, when the path had suddenly forked. Hoping to catch sight of him she followed this path for a few seconds until she was able to cut across the woods and find her brother.

Just as she thought her lungs would burst, Ned pulled up to bend and suck in air. He looked round, panting. "We've lost him, Soph."

"I am afraid so, love. There are too many paths he could have taken." Sophy shook her head. "Was he the same fellow we followed the other night, do you think?"

Ned shrugged. "Could be. He seemed shorter and rounder, though."

"Well, Sherwood has him safe now," sighed Sophy, "though in truth, Neddy, what the two of us would have done with him had we caught up to him is more than I can fathom." She giggled.

Her brother chuckled with her. "We might have had a look at him."

"Hmmm. There is that. Well, it is time we went home and you were given to Mr.Grimms."

"Oh," sighed Ned.

Twenty

Lady Anne's smart, chocolate-brown barouche pulled up in Cortland Abbey's wide courtyard. A lackey came to pull open the carriage door, unfold the steps and put out his bent arm to aid the lady's descent.

As Anne's dainty blue slipper touched the first step, she looked up at the impressive stone facade with its arched dark oak double doors. She could remember how she had dreamed of being mistress of the Abbey when she was just a girl and attracted to Chase Cortland. However, as second in line, Chase could not have made her the mistress of Cortland. His brother, Roland, had been the earl at that time. Then Bartholomew, that rich, rich man, came along and Roland's comfortable living was nought. Bartholomew's estate, though smaller in size and stature than the Abbey, was certainly pretty, and Bartholomew had fortune enough to allow her far more rein than Roland would have been able to manage. She had carefully weighed the situation, even then at seventeen.

She moved toward the large, arched, oak double doors. Woodly opened them wide and inclined his head. Anne smiled to herself. It would be such a pleasure to decorate and furnish this place for herself with Chase's fortune. What a very fashionable couple they would make.

"Anne, dear," Lucinda appeared in the Great Hall and came down its wide length with her hand extended.

The two women exchanged kisses in the air as they bent toward one another, but it was Lucinda who was in command. "Come, Chase is not home yet, which will afford us a cozy chat in the meantime."

"Not at home?" Anne became pettish at once and made no attempt to hide her displeasure. "But he knew I was coming."

"Yes, dear, and I am certain he has been unavoidably detained. No doubt, he will appear at any moment. Never mind, the servants have been hard at work cleaning and polishing my dear sister's little sitting room. I think we may be comfortable there. It has a wonderful view of the rose garden."

Anne wasn't in the mood for garden views. She wanted the earl, but she put on a pleasant enough face and allowed Lucinda to take her off.

The earl had purposely taken the long way home from his solicitor's office in town. He wanted to walk in late on Lady Anne. He wanted her to become impatient with waiting for him. He needed an advantage, and if anyone could rattle Lady Anne, Lucinda could.

He had long ago decided exactly what Anne was, cunning and manipulative. He knew that she would arrive at Cortland with her guns loaded. However, her target would be missing and knowing Anne as he was sure he now did, this would throw her off balance with frustration. He was fairly certain that Anne had made up her mind to be Lady Cortland. He knew it was his fortune that had seduced her to this decision. She meant to hold his land hostage, but there was the outside chance that he could beat her at her own game. To win, he needed to be in control of the negotiations. He would have to stoop to her level and allow her to think that he was interested in her once more. He had learned long ago to stay one step ahead of the devil. That was precisely why he had gone to visit young Harcot this morning and between them they had devised a plan.

"Faith, I can't believe how far we came." Sophy looked around with exasperation. "Drat! I have lost my shawl, my lovely new shawl. It must have gotten caught somewhere. I shall have to recall what paths we took if I am ever to find it and I must find it." This last was said on a forlorn note, for it was the shawl the earl had given her. The notion of it being lost was like a black cloud hanging overhead.

"I'll find it for you, Soph, after my lessons," offered her brother as they stepped out onto the open road.

"Oh no, you are not coming back here alone, do you hear me Ned Egan?" Sophy's hands were picking at a stem of briar attached to her mass of tangled red tresses so that she did not see the approaching horse and rider.

"Ho!" chuckled the earl as he pulled his horse up. "What the deuce are you two up to now?"

"My lord!" cried Ned joyfully. He moved beside the earl's horse and reached up to stroke the beast's huge muscular neck as he proceeded to bring the earl up to date. "We have just had a bang-up time! I had been thinking all night and came up with a notion. We went out this morning to test it, and my lord, *I* was right! That fellow with the lantern is very clever. He backtracked. I found his print on the south side of the stream. Soph and I," he leaned and, in an aside, confided, "Soph came after me you see, because of Grimms and now she is very cross because she lost the shawl you gave her. But never mind all that for just as the prints came to a dead stop at the bottom of a hill, there he was!"

"There who was?" The earl was frowning.

"A round, little fellow in a peaked cap. He looked to be watching us, but when he realized that we saw him, off he went. We gave chase, but we lost him and here we are."

The earl dismounted his horse and inclined his head at Miss Egan who was blushing beautifully. He thought even in her disarray that she was the loveliest woman on earth. His blue eyes twinkled. "And so here you are. I can understand Ned taking off after the scoundrel, but I had thought, Miss Egan that *you* would have better sense?"

Temper came to Sophy's rescue. Forgotten was the kiss, Lady Anne and her own confused emotions. Hands went to her hips. "He ran, we followed. I was hoping to get a look at him, after all, he might be King Ludd." Her chin was up. "No harm was done."

"Even a rabbit when cornered will bare its teeth, little girl," he said softly, even as the gaze of his blue eyes caressed her.

Her emotions returned and flooded her cheeks with color. "We did not corner him."

"Besides," put in Ned with a shrug. "I don't really think he is King Ludd."

"Don't you, my man?" smiled the earl. "Nor do I."

"Who then is he, do you think?" Sophy's delicate brow was up.

"Branden's Bow Street Runner," answered the earl.

"By Jove, yes," agreed Ned excitedly. "Of course, I should have known."

The earl laughed. "Indeed, now how many Bow Street Runners have you known? Off with you. Poor Mr. Grimms awaits!"

They bid one another good-day and the earl watched them for a moment before he walked his horse into the woods, tethered him and retraced the path Sophy and Ned had made during their charge through the woods. This proved to be an easy task as the headstrong pair had trampled everything in their way while they had raced over low bushes and thick weed growth. It didn't take long for the earl to find what he was looking for, return to his horse, and make his way to the Abbey. He was certain that by now both Lucinda and Lady Anne were ready to draw blood—each other's, and no doubt his as well!

Twenty-one

The earl had been right on the mark when he assumed that Lady Anne would be out of sorts at his tardy arrival. He reached the Abbey nearly forty minutes late, to find Lucinda chiding Lady Anne for her pettiness as she escorted her down the length of the Great Hall to the front door.

Both ladies turned to glare at him as he casually handed his beaver top hat and well worn riding gloves to his butler. "Ah, forgive me. I am late, I know. It could not be helped, but I knew my aunt would keep you company, Anne." He reached for and took her hand, although she had not extended it to him.

He looked at her in a way all his own, and, at his most charming, said softly, "I can see that you are annoyed with me, sweet goddess, but I am here now. Can I not make it up to you?"

Lucinda was out of patience with Anne and more than a little irritated with her nephew. He had said he would only be ten or fifteen minutes late! Nearly an hour in Anne's company alone had been enough to make her wish the woman in Hades. She folded her arms across her middle now to say, "Anne may find it in her to forgive you, darling, but I do not!"

"No? Come along you two, what we need is a luncheon. I am ravenous and so must both of you be as well."

Anne was very certain he was the most handsome man she had contemplated in many a month. His boyish charm was certainly appealing and she *was* hungry. Lucinda was overbearing and a tiresome witch who she was very sure did not like her. But, no matter. When she married the earl, Lucinda would be of no account. She had managed to maintain her temper today with the earl's aunt, but once they were married it would be quite a different story. So she put on a sweet smile and said, "Of course, if you have a good reason for being late?"

"It won't be good enough for me," said Lucinda turning on her heel and going toward the dining room. "I shall have luncheon served immediately!"

"There you are!" breathed Harry as he strode across the Egans' front lawn, with Oscar close on his heels, to meet Sophy and Ned. "We were just on our way to search you two out."

"Why?" laughed Sophy taking his extended hand in both hers and giving them a friendly squeeze.

"Why? Why she asks," Harry snorted to no one in particular.

"Your household is in something of an uproar," interjected Oscar by way of an explanation. "Apparently your father, as you must know, went off early this morning." He frowned over this and sighed, "Seems to me your father should be around a bit more." Then he saw that Sophy was about to rebuke him and hurriedly went on, "Yes, well. There was Grimms in something of a tither and threatening to walk out. Packed his bags and started ranting about young Ned."

"Loyal staff you've got there," interjected Harry. "Took offense."

"Cook seems to have threatened him with her rolling pin, and a housemaid advised him that she would bar the door with her body if need be until you had returned."

"Stendly nearly had an apoplexy," added Harry with a chuckle. "That's when we walked onto the scene."

"And, by this time, everyone was ducking Cook's rolling pin. It was a regular set to, with everyone shouting at the same time." Oscar shook his head. "So there you are. And that is why we were coming to find you!"

"Well, that about sums up the matter right and tight." Sophy was greatly amused by the scene this presented in her mind's eye. She clucked her tongue as she quickly thought the matter over. "Well, there is certainly no cause for all this nonsense." She eyed her brother as they entered their front door. "It is time, I think, to give Grimms his walking papers. He does not after all, exhibit a desire to remain with us at Egan. What say you, Neddy?"

"Famous! Can I watch you give him the boot?" Neddy's face was alight with expectation.

"No, I don't think that would be nice. Boot, indeed," said Sophy.

At her back Oscar leaned toward Ned to whisper, "Fusty old fellow, this Grimms. Glad to see him go."

"Time was Neddy was at Harrow," added Harry, thinking that looking out for Sophy and her sibling was becoming a life's work.

Neddy heard these words with a grimace. "Wish m'father felt that way. No doubt he will send for another tutor who will turn out to be some antiquated old fidget, worse even than Grimms!"

They entered the house to find Bessy, true to her word,

blocking Mr. Grimms' path with an impassioned, "Ye can not leave until ye speak wit Miss Egan, sir."

"Thank you, Bess, Mr. Grimms may speak with me now." Sophy smiled warmly at Bess Cornes and turned an uplifted brow at Mr. Grimms. "What, sir, leaving without notice, without bidding my father farewell? I consider that very untoward behavior, both rude and disrespectful. I can not think why you would wish to blot your record and references with such unprofessional behavior."

"As to that, my record is in better standing than yours!" retorted Mr. Grimms testily, though he flushed nearly purple with his discomfort.

"He wants his cork drawn," seethed Harry, taking offense on Sophy's behalf.

"What a very nasty remark," Sophy frowned at Mr. Grimms. "I must attribute it to your irrational agitation."

"I am not irrational, Miss Egan, and I am not stupid. I know what is going on." He pointed at Bess. "The fact that you have people such as *she* working in your home displays in which direction *your* connections run. Your brother is allowed to run amok in Sherwood Forest where I can imagine what sort of criminal elements he hobnobs with at all hours of the day and night. Though blame should be laid at your father's door, since his violent views are touted in his essays. Wicked, wicked. I will not live in a den of treasonous Luddites!"

"How dare you!" Sophy flushed with sudden rage. She nearly found herself bringing up her hand to slap his face, but she got control of herself. She had no notion what he could be talking about. She had been amazed at his reference to Bess, astounded at his preposterous assumptions about her young brother's activities and thoroughly outraged at his reference to her father. Her mind felt nearly frozen with rage. Her parent's many essays were about the rights of Englishmen, about the rights of mankind. They were not about violence, riots, or treason! She was evidently dealing with a lunatic.

Cook had gasped at Grimms' effrontery. Stendly stood with fists clenched and ready, but poor Ned, who had been dumbfounded, suddenly came to life. He would have landed Mr. Grimms a neat kick to the shin, had not Harry caught and held him in check. Ned settled for hissing instead. "Bleater! Don't you ever say a word against my father!"

"Ned, hush," objected his sister. "Mr. Grimms is obviously unwell and unaware of the seriousness of his false accusations." She turned to glare at the tutor.

"He is a bloody piece of Haymarket ware!" Harry pronounced and pointed dramatically to the front door. "Out! Out, I say! It is only the presence of a lady that forbids my telling you in very precise terms what you can do with yourself." Harry wasn't sure what all this was about, but the aristocrat in him was greatly shocked at the servant's attitude.

"Stendly, show Mr. Grimms the door," requested Oscar at his haughtiest. He was greatly shocked at Mr. Grimms' remarks and at his disrespectful attitude. People were taking heated sides over the Luddites, but Oscar was taken aback by Grimms' suggestion that having sympathy for the Luddites was next to treason. He was, as was Harry, an Englishman, do or die.

Stendly was quick to go to the door, and betrayed his emotions by opening it wide with something of a flourish. Grimms, however, glanced at the door disdainfully before he addressed Sophia.

"I assume one of your people will be good enough to drive me to town where I shall be taking the stage in the morning," he managed to request with his chin still in the air.

"Let the blackguard walk!" Harry demanded, for he was incensed beyond mercy.

"I can not, Harry," said Sophy, wishing that she could. "Indeed, we were kind enough to send a gig to bring the fellow to Egan. That is how we must send him off." Sophy looked at the man coldly. "Wait here a moment, sir." She left then and went to her library where she hurriedly scribbled a note for her head groom. She then collected a full month's wage for the tutor, though he had only worked a week out of it, and returned to the hall, where she handed both items to him. "Good-by Mr. Grimms."

"And good riddance!" Ned nearly spat. "You weren't worth a *sou* as a tutor. If you had been, I would have spent more time in the schoolroom. As it was, I had more to learn anywhere else but with you."

"Well put, Ned, well put," approved Oscar.

Finally Grimms was gone and Sophy looked to Cook and Stendly to quietly dismiss them with a warm thank you. However, she did detain Bess to softly say, "Bess, I am so sorry if anything that man said offended you."

"No, miss, he was only speaking the truth," Bess answered with lowered eyes.

"Nonsense," said Sophy.

"It is true. Ye see m'Johhny be a weaver over at Branden Mills and well, things be, er, in a muddle." She couldn't tell them that Johnny was entrenched in the Luddite movement. However, she didn't have to. It was immediately understood.

Oscar gave a low whistle and Harry said, "We better go to your library, Soph and have a little talk."

Twenty-two

Nathan Walker had witnessed Lady Anne's arrival. He knew that the earl had not returned to the Abbey and decided to time his next move with precision.

He calculated carefully as he watched the masons finish the last ornamental stonework round the waterfall they had been in the process of renovating in the Japanese Gardens. As he looked around, he felt a sure satisfaction. His architectural design was flawless, and he knew that when the gardeners finished with the landscaping, the view of stonework, shrubbery, and cascading water would be breathtaking. He smiled to himself. Indeed, Sophy would be in awe of his work and he decided it was time he fetched her. She had expressed a desire to have a look at this project. He smiled to himself for he could think of no better opportunity. There was no doubt in his mind that when the earl arrived he would take Lady Anne on a tour of the gardens.

It took him only fifteen minutes total to saddle his horse and make the short ride to Egan Grange. There he was much at ease, leaving his horse outside the front steps with a boy as he waved Stendly off, saying he would announce himself.

Sophy had only minutes before waved off Harry and Oscar after having taken part, as an interested listener, in an exhausting diatribe on the perfidy of disloyal servants.

Both men decided they would ride to town and have a
look in at what the miserable Grimms was about. Oscar
had it in his head that the man meant to make mischief.
Sophy found this notion rather farfetched, but was affectionately moved by their sincere concern for her family.

She realized that she was famished and took a moment
to gulp down tea and biscuits before attending to the business of charting out a needed program of study for her
tutorless brother who was pulling a rueful face and rolling
his eyes at her.

"What?" she demanded hands on hips.

"Soph, I am eleven, nearly twelve. I think I can manage
to read a sight more difficult book than this." He pushed
the offending childrens' history book away.

"Hallo. Am I interrupting? I told Stendly I would show
myself in." Nathan Walker stood at the study door.

Sophy regarded him with a warm smile. He had been
pleasant company last evening, and though he was not
dashing like the earl, he was certainly attractive in his
own groomed, and well-ordered style. There too, he was
a welcome diversion from the insanity of the hectic morning. "Nathan, thank goodness!" She turned to eye her
brother and said, "Why don't you decide just what you
are old enough to read and then stick to it for the next
two hours. Is that fair, my buck?"

"Done!" agreed Ned happily. He was pleased enough
to find himself his own master.

"What, no Mr. Grimms close on his heels this morning?" Nathan teased.

"Soph gave him the boot," answered Ned with a wide
scampish grin.

"Ned!" objected his sister who had gone forward to
give Nathan her hand. "We have had the devil of a morn-

ing. In fact, it was so bizarre, I am not at all sure it happened."

He held her hand for a long moment and in fact, did not release it until she brought her questioning green eyes up to his face.

"I tell you what, come with me for a short ride and we shall sort it all out. What say you?" He was at his most charming and Nathan Walker was very capable of charm.

Sophy did not dislike Nathan, and at that moment he was much like the man she had recalled in her girlish dreams. She was confused by her feelings for the earl, who had displayed himself as an obvious cold-hearted rake. She needed to put that confusion aside and return to steady ground. Riding would do that for her. Indeed, riding was just what she very much wanted to do. "Oh yes, I should like that. I'll just go up and change into my riding habit. I shan't be long. In the meantime, Stendly can have my mare sent up from the stables."

"I took the liberty of asking him to do just that, Sophia," Nathan returned confidently.

Sophy disliked being manipulated. She frowned over this for a moment. However, good humor won out and she laughed. "How thoughtful." Then she left the room.

Walker watched her back as she made her exit, before turning to find Ned looking at him. "Think to turn Soph up sweet, eh? It won't take, you know."

Nathan Walker took affront. He wasn't about to allow a halfling to speak impertinently to him. "I don't think it is your place to comment on such matters."

"Don't you?" retorted Ned, who was sure now that he did not like Nathan Walker. "Sophy is m'sister and therefore it is my place, more than yours!"

"I was referring to your age," said Walker witheringly.

Ned was not affected. He shrugged, "Age has nought to do with it. Know my sister a sight better than *you* do, and I know you two won't suit in the end. Zounds! Plain as pikestaff that you want a prissy creature. Soph *prissy?* And she ain't biddable. If you don't know that, you don't know Soph." He shrugged again. "So, if I were you I'd think twice about having at her."

"You are not me. You are eleven years old and though you *think* you know a great deal, Ned, in fact, you do not!" snapped Nathan.

"I'm still old enough to know m'sister!" retorted Ned. "You mean to make a push to have Soph, but she won't have you." Ned turned away from him. He had said too much, he knew, and if Sophy knew she would have his head. However, he did feel safe in the belief that his sister did not appear to him to have any romantic inclinations whatsoever toward Nathan Walker.

Nathan Walker found himself irritated beyond words and decided he would not honor Ned's last comment with a rebuttal. Instead he bid young Egan a good morning and left the room in time to meet Sophia skipping down the staircase. She looked glorious in her royal blue riding ensemble with her flaming tresses tucked in adorable curls beneath her royal blue velvet top hat with its bouncing white feather. Indeed, he thought to himself, he would be very pleased to call this creature Mrs. Walker!

At Cortland Abbey the earl attempted with some success to entertain his aunt and Lady Anne during their luncheon. It proved too much of a strain for Lucinda to handle, and she soon excused herself.

This left Lady Anne free to feel uninhibited. The pretty

woman took to stroking the earl's thigh under the table. The earl maintained his composure as he took both her hands into his and brought them to his lips. "Come beauty, 'tis time I showed you the lay of the land."

"I would rather see what you have done with the house. We could start with the bedroom." Anne's lips parted suggestively and her eyelashes coyly fluttered.

Hedley had arrived with a message for the earl from one of the gardeners in time to witness this, and raised his elfin chin as his eyes went heavenward and asked for protection from the likes of Lady Anne. He made a show of clearing his throat and when he had the earl's attention announced, "Mr. Walker left word with the head gardener that if you would like to have a look, the waterfall is ready for your inspection."

The earl knew that Hedley was greatly disturbed by Lady Anne's presence. He smiled kindly at him and said that he and his guest would be along presently.

He turned his deep blue eyes upon Anne once more and released her hand, managing to delicately indicate that it was time to rise from the dining table. "You see, there is always something ready to intervene when temptation becomes too strong. It is the difference between age and folly. Today, our play must be confined to the pleasures of the gardens, leaving the pleasures of the bedrooms for another, perhaps more discreet opportunity."

She tittered, pleased to find him receptive to her outrageous forwardness. He was right of course, no sense inviting gossip. There would be time enough to lure him into passion once she was closer to her goal. She linked her arm with his and glided alongside him as he led her to the hall where he wrapped her cloak round her delicate shoulders. A moment later found them strolling through the rose garden. Hedley watched from a lead-paned window and clucked his tongue.

"Your mare is sporting for a run, Sophia," said Nathan as he smiled to watch Sophy's horse prance in place.

"Indeed, she is a very good girl and deserves a run. Shall we give it to her, sir?" Sophy felt much in need of one herself.

It was just what Nathan had planned. With an imperceptive leg movement, and a grin over his shoulder, he and his roan gelding were moving quickly from a canter into a gallop. Sophy laughed as she gave her mare rein and followed suit. They sped in this fashion across one of Egan's grassy fields to the wall that separated Egan from Cortland land. Nathan took his fence flying, but Sophy brought her mare beneath her and took the jump smoothly. Nathan brought his horse round and trotted back toward her as she slowed her horse and patted her pretty chestnut mare's neck.

"Neatly done, Sophia, neatly done, indeed, though I have always thought you more neck or nothin'." He wanted to divert her from the fact that they were now at Cortland.

"Why, Mr. Walker, I am riding side-saddle and paying heed to the proprieties. If you want to see me take my fences flying, you must catch me when I am riding astride and in my britches!" Sophy laughed, then settled down to sigh. "Thank you, I certainly did need that." She looked round, "Oh, we are now on Cortland ground."

He shrugged. "The earl wouldn't mind. Look, we can use the bridle path that runs through Cortland Woods. It will allow us easy access to the waterfall and Japanese Garden I have been wanting to show you." He could see

Sophy hesitate. "I do so want you to see the results of my handiwork."

Sophy frowned over this. "I don't want to go anywhere near the house though. That would be so very presumptuous and I really wouldn't like the earl to find me wandering about."

"Nonsense. Wandering about, indeed. You are in my company. Besides, I have told him that I have invited you to Cortland to see my work. He was most gracious about it."

"Was he? How kind of him," said Sophy dryly. "Right then, lead on, sir."

"Oh, now this is pretty," allowed Anne as the earl led her from the rose garden into a huge area his great grandfather had named the Spanish Gardens. It was a vast arrangement of triangles and squares of neatly trimmed evergreen hedges. In the center of this close fitting puzzle was an old well around which a circle of hedging and flowers had been fetchingly designed. In the center of each hedge block were clusters of vibrantly colored flowers. The gardeners were busy at work, as there was still a great deal of planting to be completed, but the effect even in its early stages was quite enchanting.

"Indeed, seen from the ballroom, this view in spring especially is quite inspiring," said the earl softly. He was being deliberately careful with his flirtation. He wanted nothing he said to be misconstrued.

"And where does this path lead?" Anne returned as she stepped onto a bluestone walkway.

"To the Prior's Lake, fed from a spring. Again, its name and creation were due to my great-grandfather. He had a

waterfall installed and a rich landscaping of imported evergreens and shrubbery brought in especially for the Japanese Garden. It became sadly overgrown and dilapidated
over time, and fell into ruins during the last twelve years.
I had Nathan redesign its lines, keeping as close to the
original theme as was possible. I haven't seen what has
been done there in the last few days and had better do so
before Nathan takes me to task."

He could see that she was very nearly yawning, and
was not surprised, for Anne had never been interested in
such things. History and heritage were in her mind fusty
and dull. Indeed, her talk of gowns, routs, and *on-dits* held
little interest for him, and he was looking forward to meeting up with Nathan Walker if only as a diversion.

"Waterfalls, Japanese Gardens. So romantic," purred
Anne as she held tight to his large strong arm, and detained him when they reached a bend in the pathway se-
cluded by trees and tall shrubs.

"Just the sort of setting I like . . ." she whispered.

Nathan and Sophy stopped by the pond which had been
cleaned of debris. It sparkled in the sunlight. Water lilies
were budding in their pretty green leaf clusters. Shrubs
were trimmed and shapely as they swayed and hung round
the pond. The waterfall cascaded over sleek slabs of rocks
on its journey to a set of wide-angled flat slabs of rock
allowing the water to form pools on its way to the pond.

"Nathan, this is breath-taking!" Sophy loosened her
hold on her reins and allowed the mare to drop her head
to take a quick gulp of water.

"Yes, it is, I think. It adds such elegance to the grounds.
Our next project will be the chapel." He stopped as he

heard voices and felt rather victorious as he looked toward the sound.

Sophy turned as well, in time to see Lady Anne grab hold of the earl's coat lapels as she raised herself to him. Sophy could see the beautiful blond whispering something before she kissed the earl full on his mouth! For a moment, Sophy wanted to die. No doubt the lovers thought they were private. They had no idea they could be seen from horseback across the way. Sophy just managed to stifle a gasp and turned her blushing face to Nathan. "Please Nathan, I think we should slip away, quickly before they see us." Her heart was reverberating in her chest. Her vision was blurry and all at once she did not feel well. She couldn't breathe. She couldn't think. Buck up girl, she told herself. So much for his meaningless kisses. It was nought to him, it is nought to you.

Nathan took her gloved hand and said softly, "I am sorry. I had no notion he was, er, entertaining." He put her hand to his lips. "Does it so disturb you to see him with another?" There, he had put it to her. She had no choice but to deny it. It would give him a clear route for his next assault.

"Disturb *me?* Now, why in heaven's name should it?" Sophy answered on a high note. "I only meant that we should give the man his privacy, on his own land."

The earl had come away from Anne's kiss feeling very nearly sick. He had not realized how much he disliked her in every imaginable way. Something else nagged at him, and it had a name. Sophy. Being here, seducing Anne, was disturbing what he felt for Sophy. However, this was business he told himself. This was being ruthless with one who was ruthless, it had nought to do with Sophy and him. Then, all at once, he looked round and there she was! She was magnificent in her royal blue ensemble with her red tresses wildly escaping her top hat. Her green eyes flashed with shock and then anger and he took a step forward, not knowing what to say, but wanting to say something.

"Oh, for pity's sake, he has seen us!" ejaculated Sophy in some distress.

"There is nothing for it. Come Sophy, we must wave and proceed on our way. We'll go toward the front drive so that it doesn't look as though we are slinking off," said Nathan quietly. He couldn't believe his good luck. If he had written the scene he could not have done better for himself.

Nathan put up his hand and the earl, feeling like a completely inadequate idiot, put up his. There was nothing else he could do at the moment. From beneath knit brows, he watched Nathan and Sophy walk their horses away. Damnation! There was no doubt whatsoever in his mind that Sophy had witnessed Anne kissing him.

Anne tugged at his sleeve. "You are angry? I had no idea anyone would be about. We seemed so alone."

"I have learned that things are rarely what they seem." He took her gloved hand. "Come seductress, 'tis time you were on your way."

"Yes, but we didn't even talk about that piece of land you want to buy from me," Lady Anne reminded him of her ace.

"Ah, the land." He shook his head. "I am afraid I have changed my mind. I thought to buy it on a momentary whim. I have since decided I no longer want it," the earl returned, using *his* ace!

Twenty-three

Lucinda had been in a tiff. Watching her nephew flirt with Lady Anne had been more than a little irritating, particularly as she had the notion that he was enjoying himself. She began to feel concerned that he was falling into the same trap. What she needed was fresh air and a good long walk to clear her head!

She took the stone pathway that led to the Spanish Gardens, smiled sweetly at the army of gardeners, and stopped to enjoy a chat with them about the various ornamental flowers. However, she hurried down the wide stone steps to the west lawn when she heard the sound of her nephew and Lady Anne at her back. She was heartily sick of Anne's purring. She cut across to the neat woods that bordered this stretch of lawn and took a manicured path through the thicket. Walking vigorously, she was surprised to find herself, all at once, on the main road. Back-tracking to a fork in the wooded path brought her onto the Cortland drive, where she found two riders coming toward her. She knew Nathan Walker, and immediately recognized the redhead beside him as Miss Egan! Lucinda's spirits picked up all at once for no discernible reason and she smiled a warm welcome as the pair approached.

"Good afternoon, your grace," greeted Nathan with an inclination of his head. He was just a bit in awe of Lucinda, whose reputation as the leading hostess of the *ton* had caught his attention during his time in London. He smiled toward Sophy. "Allow me to introduce Miss Sophia Egan." He went on to unnecessarily explain, "The Duchess of Bellevedere is the earl's favorite aunt."

"Yes, I know," said Sophy. She smiled warmly at Lucinda as she bent to take the older woman's hand in a gentle clasp. "Hallo, I did in fact notice you at Saltash last evening, but wasn't afforded the opportunity then of making your acquaintance." Her eyes twinkled as she recalled one or two tales the earl had recounted about his favorite relative. "I have heard some very inspiring things about you. The earl speaks your name frequently and with great affection. What a great pleasure it is to meet you."

Well, thought Lucinda with feeling, here now was a girl, indeed! She liked Sophy's easy frank sweetness of manner. She liked her very natural presence and she particularly liked the twinkle in her green eyes. She beamed a friendly response as she returned the handshake and said, "That sounds most encouraging, for I doubt that he would speak of me with great affection this afternoon." She gave them both an open appraisal. "Have you been visiting with my nephew up at the house? I had not realized I was out walking that long?"

Sophy blushed and looked to Nathan to answer. Lucinda was quick to notice this and as it deftly registered in her brain and clicked off silent questions, Nathan explained in hearty accents, "Miss Egan and I were out riding and as we happened to be near the waterfall which Miss Egan rather wished to see, we rode through the back field and did not go up to the house. We did however, meet the earl and Lady Anne for a moment as they were taking a tour of the Japanese Gardens."

Sophy frowned, for while that was what had actually happened, it was not the precise truth. It was Nathan who had wished her to see the waterfall.

"I see," said Lucinda, who watched Sophy's flitting expressions during Nathan's explanation. Very little escaped the duchess' notice, but even so, she was not quite sure what to make of this new development. Something she was not at all sure of was taking place. Was this charming beauty forming a tendre for her nephew's architect? What a dreadful, awful waste. This one deserved a king, and lacking that, an earl. Besides, Lucinda had not taken to Nathan Walker. It was not that she disliked him, yet she could not quite like him either. At any rate, Lucinda had every intention of ferreting out the meaning of her observations. "Well, it is obvious too many years in India has allowed my nephew to forget English manners. I however, have not. Please allow me to insist that you come up to the house for some refreshment. Please do come."

Sophy was quick to answer, "I am afraid I can not. My father is not home today and has left a desk full of letters for me to attend to in his absence. Thank you." She smiled warmly. "You are most welcome to visit us at the Grange, your grace, and I hope you will do so very soon."

"Indeed, child, you may count on it," answered Lucinda as she waved them off. She watched them trot off for a moment before walking toward the house. As she reached the front courtyard she was in time to witness her nephew kissing Lady Anne's gloved hand before closing her carriage door. A moment later she was giving Anne a brief smile as her barouche passed, before she turned to stomp dangerously toward the earl.

"Chase Cortland, I mean to have a word with you!"

***

Nathan and Sophy rode for a few moments in silence. He did not realize that she was not interested in making conversation with him because he was deep in thought himself. He was hurriedly reviewing the results of his morning's efforts and smugly patting himself on the back.

He would have been astounded to know that he had done himself harm in Sophy's eyes. The episode gravely irritated her and gave her pause for doubt. *She* had not asked to see the waterfall. Nathan had teased her into it. She had not liked the notion of going to Cortland uninvited by the earl himself, and she had been right. Just look what had happened! She had felt a fool and worse, so much worse.

The earl, or rather the earl and Lady Anne, had thought they were private, though how they could have thought so with gardeners popping in and out all over the place was more than she could fathom. She sighed sadly putting a lost hope aside. The earl and Lady Anne were lovers. The thought made her feel as though her heart was being prodded with unfeeling fingers. This had to stop. Then, all at once, Nathan was reining in his horse and reaching for her gloved hand and she was wishing him at Jericho!

"Sophy, do you know how I feel about you?" His voice was low and husky.

Her lashes flashed and color flooded her cheeks. "Of course. We are friends, dear, dear friends." Were they? Had they ever been? Oscar and Harry were her friends. Harry was attempting to court her, but his methods were open and honest. Instinct told her that Nathan's were not.

He nearly snorted, but controlled himself. "It is a start, the best of starts."

"Nathan," she cut him off hurriedly and behaved as though she did not realize where his words were attempting to take her, "It is so very late. Do you think we could pick up the pace. I simply must hurry home. I had thought I would not be gone above an hour and nearly two have passed."

He realized now was not the time. He needed to woo her in a more romantic setting, when she had less on her mind. "Of course, my dear. Off we go," he said urging his horse into a quiet lope.

"Chase, I should like a word with you," said Lucinda in a tone meant to convey the fact that she would not be put off.

The earl was gravely distressed. He was certain that Sophy had witnessed Anne kissing him. He was a sophisticated man of two-and-thirty and had no business worrying about schoolboy nonsense. No business at all, and yet he was very nearly heartsick at what Sophy might think. "Of course. What is it, Lucy love?" he asked in less than enthusiastic terms.

Lucinda's brow went up. "Did things not go well with Anne the Grasping?"

He laughed out loud, but it had a hollow sound. "As to that, yes, things went exactly as we hoped they would."

"What happened then? And don't try to fob me off, Chase. *Something* has you in the suds."

"Nothing," he answered on a cool note, hoping to warn her off for the present.

"It has something to do with that Egan girl, doesn't it?" she demanded. "I didn't attain my years in society without learning a thing or two, my buck. So out with it and don't pitch any gammon for I won't have it."

He was astonished enough by her use of cant to let down his guard a measure. "What are you talking about?" His words gave away nothing but the look in his blue eyes betrayed him.

"I met her just a little while ago. She was riding with Nathan Walker, who behaved as though she were his own private property. A pity if that little romance were to take. She would be wasted on such as he." There, she had dropped her bait.

"What are you talking about? Nathan and Sophy?" The earl nearly spluttered. "I *don't* think so!"

"So, that is where the wind blows, eh, my boy?" said Lucinda softly.

He offered her his arm. "I think the wind is blowing and 'tis cold, too cold to stand out here, dearest Aunt."

Lucinda allowed the conversation to drop, but she smiled to herself.

Twenty-four

It was a dreary morning. A low mist hung about in clumps over the lawn and could be seen winding its way through the nearby thicket from the window in the study at Egan Grange. Miles Egan turned away from the eerie view to consider his daughter. He could see that she was distraught as she gave him a rendition of Mr. Grimms' odd behavior the previous morning.

Sophy's father watched her as she paced and attempted to quietly calm her by interjecting a sympathetic word here and there throughout her diatribe. However, this was counteracted by his son who stuck in a few caustic comments of his own. Sophy eyed her patient father with a touch of exasperation before uttering her conclusion. "And what the horrid fellow could have meant about treason, I have no earthly notion!"

"Nor should you worry your pretty head over such things," said her father gently.

"Not worry my pretty head?" She stamped her foot at him. "That won't do, Father. You raised me better than that and well you know it! Not worry my pretty head, indeed!"

She only called him father in stiff terms when she was at odds with him. He smiled to himself. She was so like her mother in stature, and yet worlds apart in character.

Her mother had been a gentle, ethereal creature and Sophy was a spitfire. She would forgive no trespass, and Grimms had certainly trespassed. It was time to tell Sophy something of what was going on. It was true, he had not raised her to sit quietly with stitchery. In his loneliness he had indulged himself with the pleasure of her lively company, discussing all manner of philosophies, religion, and politics with her. The net result was that she had a quick mind and ready understanding of such matters. He was, in fact, quite proud of her wit and intelligence and often relied on her clear-sighted opinions. However, Sophy was the sort who would not give things a rest until the problem at hand was completely dissected and resolved. He sighed sadly, for he did not want Sophy involved in this particular situation. Then he eyed his son, who sat there ready to defend his sister's rights. He loved his children, and he liked them as well. The time had come for them to know something about his personal politics. He went to his large winged chair and sat heavily. "Well, you two, I don't suppose you will leave this in my hands?"

"No, Papa, it has become a family matter," Sophy responded quietly, taking up a place on the yellow print sofa with her brother.

"Family matters do rest under the jurisdiction of the father." Mr. Egan made one last attempt at control.

Sophy knew how to work her will. "However, this does not affect only you, Papa. Besides, you were not here and it was *I* who had to manage an ugly situation. It is only fair that I know why it was ugly, why the word treason was used."

"Evidently I have been remiss in my parental duties. I do beg your pardon, Sophy." Miles Egan grew red-cheeked. He was always caught off-guard by Sophy's frankness. She had a direct magic all her own that opened his eyes with a snap and tugged on his hidden heart-strings. "As you say, you took the brunt of an uncomfortable situation while I was not available, and like so many other times, what should have been my job fell on your shoulders." Sophy blushed and hastened to reassure him. "Papa, please, do not misunderstand. I was not complaining. I meant only that—"

"Well, you have every right to complain. I had not meant for you to be burdened by my oversights. I should have seen this coming. I should have listened to Ned. He tried to tell me that he could not like Grimms." He shook his head. "You have every right to know what directly affects you and your brother."

"Dearest Papa, what is it? Just what is all this about?" Sophy reached over to touch his knee.

"It is about the need for reforms in our country. When I gave my proposed speech to Mr. Grimms, I thought I was merely extending a courtesy. He had on more than one occasion expressed a wish to read my political essays. It never occurred to me that he would have a reactionary nature and hold the view that I was a dangerous radical. Apparently, however, that seems to be what he concluded. Treason, indeed!"

There was something her father was holding back. Sophy realized this because she knew him so well. He was not an accomplished liar, and there was the hint of a lie in his shaded eyes.

"You mean *that* is what he meant by treason?" Sophy's green eyes opened wide with doubt.

"The fellow is addle-brained," concluded Ned in some disgust. "Always thought so."

From the doorway, Stendly announced in stentorian terms, "The Duchess of Bellevedere, the Earl of Cortland."

Sophy nearly jumped, but was given a moment to recover as Ned quickly moved across the room to welcome the earl and find himself warmly introduced to the earl's aunt. The earl looked to Sophy and said softly, "I understand that you and my aunt met one another yesterday, so I am cheated of the pleasure of introducing the two of you, and must be satisfied—"

"With me," smiled Miles Egan as he went forward to take Lucinda's gloved fingers and give them a perfunctory kiss. "I am delighted to meet you, your grace, I have often heard praise of you from many of our mutual friends, and have long hoped for the opportunity to make your acquaintance."

Lucinda immediately drew him into conversation which allowed the earl to join Sophy at her corner of the sofa. He asked softly for permission to sit beside her. She gave it reluctantly. "Good morning, Miss Egan," he said lightly, aware that she was nearly frozen with tenseness. "This is for you." He felt like a damn schoolboy. This was preposterous!

"I, I can not repeatedly accept gifts from you, my lord. It is unseemly," she answered as the color flooded her pretty cheeks.

She was the most adorable woman he had ever encountered. An emerald ribbon gathered a collection of her red tresses at the top of her head, these ringlets toppled over the remaining curls which cascaded in pretty profusion round her piquant face. She wore a morning gown of emerald green which had a heart-shaped neckline trimmed in ivory lace. The same lace trimmed the long, fitted sleeves at the cuffs, and was picked up in three rows at the hem of her gown. She presented quite an enchanting picture and the earl found himself succumbing to her charms against all his best advice.

Ned had observed the adults for a moment and then quietly withdrew from the room, correctly assuming this was his opportunity to escape. He wanted to explore the attic before his sister set him at his desk.

"This is not a gift, it's yours." The earl placed the ivory wrapped package with its pretty blue ribbon on her lap.

"Mine? Now what game is this, my lord?" Sophy's green eyes flashed. What a rogue he was to be sure.

"Open it," he urged gently.

She eyed him skeptically for a moment and he said softly, "Don't doubt me, Sophy love. I am not trying to deceive you."

She looked away from his clear blue eyes then, and did in fact undo the ribbon to expose her lost shawl. She cooed with great and undisguised pleasure, "My shawl! Oh, you have found my shawl."

"Yes, you seemed distressed about losing it. After you and Ned left me at the forest's edge, I went in and followed the trail you two had left behind. I found it in a bush of briars. I would have brought it to you immediately, but I wanted my housekeeper to try and freshen it up a bit first."

She could have hugged him. Instead, her lashes brushed her cheek and as she raised her green eyes to him she said quietly, "I do heartily thank you. I love this shawl."

"Then, *I* thank you," he said, as he brought her hand to his lips.

Sophy became indignant as she thought, he is Lady Anne's lover. He is without conscience, without shame. He sits here and flirts with me as though it were the most natural thing to do. How dare he? Sophy's green eyes took on a brilliant glitter all at once as she advised him, "You do that so well. Are you not afraid of turning a green country girl's head? It would not be nice, and I had thought better of you, my lord."

He laughed. "You may be a country girl, but it is obvious no one can take advantage of *you*. Your eyes are wide open and your instincts are on the alert." He held her hand still in his strong grasp. "But Sophy, don't cloud your very sharp instincts. You know when a man is in earnest, as I am, don't you?" The earl had caught her attention with that, and in fact, couldn't believe he had said it, but he had. Was he mad?

Sophy got up abruptly from the sofa giving him no further opportunity to play his games with her. She joined Lucinda and her father in their conversation as best she could. A moment later the earl left the sofa to stand quietly within their circle, and though he did not speak directly to her again, his eyes and his lips smiled sweetly, ever so sweetly in her direction.

Twenty-five

"Harry, there he is again. Devil take the little runt! Damn, if he isn't meaning to talk to that blackguard, Grimms." Oscar had been moved out of his habitual state of calm into some very real agitation over the events of the last twenty-four hours. His chin pointed in the direction of a short, round man with a bushy mustache wearing a dark, wool peaked cap pulled low over his balding head, and a dark blue coat that hung almost to his boot heels. The little man had crossed the cobblestone street with his hand up in the air as he called to Grimms who was just about to climb into the standing stagecoach.

"That's the blasted runner Branden brought in, saw him watching Grimms last night at the Red Hart, when the curst fidget was in his cups." Harry frowned darkly. "Now, what do you suppose a Bow Street Runner would want with a tutor?"

"That's the thing, Harry, he ain't just a tutor is he? He was *Ned's* tutor and he has left the Egans under a black cloud, hasn't he?"

"Just so," Harry agreed on a sigh. "Don't like this, Oscar, don't like it at all."

"There is no saying what the devil the fellow was bleating on about." Oscar shook his head in some indignation. "Didn't think tutors got dead drunk, did you Harry?"

"No, I didn't and they shouldn't," agreed Harry a bit self-righteously, "but the thing is he *did* get bosky and could have said any number of ugly things to those cox-combs he was seated with last night. There is no telling what they repeated and the runner might have picked up."

"That's a fact," sighed Oscar. At that moment they observed the Bow Street Runner take out his little black note-book from an inner pocket and they watched him scribble as Grimms, filled with self-importance answered his questions.

"Well, there is nothing for it now. We had best ride to Egan straight off and tell Sophy what is toward. Poor child, as though she doesn't have enough to deal with." Harry shook his head over the problem. "Know what Oscar?"

"What Harry?"

"Don't know. That's what, but wish we were well out of it."

"Aye," sighed Oscar, "Sophy's friends, though. Stand buff."

"That's the ticket. Come on then."

"The thing is should we stay and keep an eye on the runner? After all, what can Sophy do just yet? Naught. She'd be better served if we kept an eye to Bow Street, what say you?" asked Oscar on second thought.

Harry considered this for a moment before linking his arm through Oscar's to say, "Aye, good notion, that, old fellow. We'll investigate the investigator!" he grinned at his closest friend. "You know Oscar, you are a great deal smarter than most give you credit for."

Oscar blushed and mumbled something incoherent, but was much gratified all the same. Now in perfect harmony, they took up a slow stroll while they kept a wary eye on Branden's runner.

* * *

Bess Cornes had come to town to collect a small order of household supplies for Cookie. She was at the market, waiting for these to be placed in the back of the open trap, when she noticed Grimms walking toward the stagecoach. She then saw the man her husband had pointed out as the Bow Street Runner call out to Grimms. Without hesitation she scurried across the street and set herself near the stage just out of sight, but close enough to hear some of the conversation taking place between the two men. She gasped at what she heard and with sure purpose hurried back to her trap. Without waiting for the entire order, she whipped up the horses and set their noses on the road to the Grange.

Neddy looked out the attic window and saw the earl as he helped his aunt into their carriage. Hurriedly, he opened the window and called down to Cortland to wait. The earl looked up with a rueful smile and nodded. He turned to his aunt, and shrugged. "Forgive me, Lucy, just another minute. The boy and I have become friends you see."

"Of course, darling," she answered absently. It had become apparent during their visit that her nephew and Sophia Egan were absolutely perfect for one another. However, it was also obvious that a rift had occurred between them. She was determined to repair the damage so that nature could take its course. She did not at all mind a moment to herself and sat back against the luxurious upholstered squabs to think.

Ned scampered outdoors and Lucinda winced to see that he was hampered by a club foot. She had not noted this earlier. She could see the lad obviously adored the earl. Her attention was caught and she watched quietly as Ned smiled brightly at the earl before pulling at his sleeve as he nearly exploded with the urgency of his news.

"Please, please, my lord, I need to tell you something at once."

Cortland's brow went up for there was something in Ned's voice, something in the boy's eyes that riveted his attention. This was serious. He excused himself and walked away from the carriage as he took the lad aside. "What is it, halfling?"

"I think papa is in over his head. Sophy thinks so too. I could tell she didn't quite believe him this morning," said Ned in way of explanation.

"Perhaps you should start at the beginning," the earl smiled as he held the boy's shoulder.

"Oh, that's right. You don't know about Grimms."

"About your tutor? What about your tutor?"

Ned hurriedly went on to recount the events of the previous morning. He described Grimms' odd behavior and quoted the tutor's parting accusation of treason, summing it up with his father's inadequate explanation. Out of breath and nervous he was surprised when the earl responded by saying, "So, that explains it."

"Explains what, my lord?"

"I happened to be at the Red Hart in town last evening and had the felicity of watching your tutor become foxed." He purposely did not mention the bits and pieces of the conversation he had overheard or the fact that he had noticed the runner's keen interest in Grimms.

"Grimms in his cups?" Ned was astounded. "Didn't think the fusty fidget had it in him."

The earl laughed. "Never mind, scamp. Do me the favor

of staying out of trouble for the time being and leaving
this matter in my hands."

"I thought it was beyond my ken I and I don't want
Sophy hurt."

"No, nor do I," the earl said softly. "Good lad, you may
trust me in this."

"I know that," said Ned grinning as he walked with the
earl back to the coach and stuck his red-haired head in the
door to smile apologetically at the duchess. "I do beg your
pardon, your grace," Ned said politely, "I didn't mean to
keep you waiting so long."

"Nonsense. That is what men do, keep the ladies waiting." Lucinda winked at him.

A moment later the coach was pulling away from Egan
Grange and Lucinda regarded her nephew. "Well?"

He sighed. "I am not keeping secrets, Lucy. This is a
delicate matter and I am not yet certain just what I am
dealing with here. I have a notion, a very uncomfortable
notion, that troubled waters lay straight ahead."

"For the Egans you mean, darling?" Lucinda looked at
him.

He met her gaze with a rueful smile. "Fishing, Lucy
love?" He then relented and added before she had time
to give him a sharp retort, "Yes, for the Egans. Tonight
my troubles should be on the mend, that is if you have
managed Hester?"

"Managed Hester, indeed," scoffed Lucinda. "No one
manages Hester. However, she is very happy to oblige. In
fact, she is looking forward to what she calls the games!"

The earl shook his head. "Then, Lucy love, 'let the
games begin!' "

Twenty-six

The mid-afternoon sun and a brisk spring breeze had dispersed the morning's fog. However, a scattering of clouds moving through the greyish sky obscured the sun's warmth, and Sophy held her shawl tightly round her shoulders as she leaned against the sturdy rails of the paddock fence. She and her brother watched his new foal, Intrepid, at play.

The young colt was certainly a beauty, with a bright white star on his forehead and four white stockings. Ned and Sophy laughed to see him jump and kick, lose his balance and defiantly throw his lovely head about, while his mother grazed quietly nearby.

"He is going to stand seventeen hands like his father," pronounced Ned happily.

Sophy grimaced. "Then he will be too much horse for you, my bucko!" She nodded toward the next paddock where Ned's pony stuck his head over the fence to watch the colt's antics.

"Think Bouncer is jealous?" she teased.

Ned laughed. "No, he'll be pleased as punch to spend the rest of his days put out to pasture, won't you, my devil?"

Bouncer snorted, turned his back on the colt and its mother, and returned to his grazing. Ned laughed again and shook his head. "See?"

At that moment Sophy's attention was caught by a rider coming up their front drive and as she realized who it was she pulled a face and sighed. "Oh dear, nowhere to hide. I am fairly caught."

Ned looked in the direction of her gaze and rubbed his nose. "Don't like Nathan Walker as much as you once did, eh, Soph?"

"Well, I am not sure that is precisely it. I am just not in the mood for company, I suppose."

Nathan Walker waved from his horse's back and Sophy put on a welcoming smile to return the salutation as her brother teased, "Well, you've got it." He laughed and dashed off for the stable to fetch a treat for his foal's mother.

Nathan pulled to a halt just before he reached the grassy paddock and dismounted. He threw the reins over his horse's head and led him the remainder of the distance to Sophy, where he allowed him to graze. "Good afternoon, Miss Egan," he said as he took her ungloved fingers to his lips.

"It is, isn't it?" smiled Sophy, "I suppose we have the wind to thank for it." She eyed him curiously. "I don't suppose your men were able to get much accomplished this morning in the drizzling rain we had?"

"On the contrary. Though we have renovated any number of rooms, we still have enough work indoors to keep us busy on days such as these." He chuckled for a moment before adding, "The place is so devoid of furniture that I suppose Lady Anne and the earl will soon start shopping. He will need hangings for all those windows."

"Really? I would have thought the earl might choose to do that with his aunt?"

"Yes, so did I, but then I heard something last evening that finally made sense." He clicked his tongue. "I had wondered just how Lady Anne and the earl had become

so close, so quickly, after all, he has been in India the last
twelve years?" He leaned closer to Sophy and said in a
confidential tone, "Apparently it was the Lady Anne you
see, all those years ago. She was the woman that the earl
and his late brother fought a duel over." He let his words
sink in and had the satisfaction of seeing their impact
almost immediately.

If Walker had struck her it could not have done more
damage. Sophy's mouth dropped, and her heart fell into
her stomach. That settled that. Lady Anne was his true love.
All hope was dashed! Sophy was not even able to make a
show of composure. Her hand fluttered to shade her eyes.

"What, what is it, Sophia?" Walker saw her face go
white and wondered if he had gone too far too soon.

"Naught. But Nathan, I am not feeling quite the thing.
Please excuse me. I, I think I will just go up to the house
and lie down." Sophy took a step away from him. Why
had he come? To eliminate the competition by breaking
her heart? Well, then. The earl belonged to Lady Anne,
but she would not belong to Nathan Walker. Suddenly she
had to leave.

"Yes, of course. Shall I walk with you?"

Sophy was already rushing off and with a movement
of her hand, as though to ward him off, she added in a
scarcely audible voice, "Thank you, no."

This was all becoming too much for her. Her father
was keeping the truth from her and it was a truth she had
every right to know. Instinct told her this. Instinct told her
their family name was in jeopardy and she was momentarily powerless to do anything about it.

Then, just as she was beginning to think that perhaps
she was wrong about Lady Anne and the earl, *this!* How
could it be true? Had he not looked at her with feeling

this morning? Had he not kissed her with feeling? Yet, this was proof. Her mind immediately accepted Nathan's words as completely true. That was why people had whispered when they looked toward the Lady Anne and the earl at the rout. The earl and Anne had a history, a history of true love . . . and on this last thought, Sophy's tears trickled down her cheeks.

Ned had quietly squeezed between the rails to enter the paddock with a carrot extended toward his foal's mother. He smiled as she bit off a large piece, but his attention was caught when he heard the earl's name coupled with Lady Anne's. He stood and watched as his sister ran off in some agitation. She wasn't sick! At least she hadn't been sick before Nathan Walker had arrived and told his tales about the earl. Well, though he was eleven, he wasn't blind and he wasn't stupid! All at once, Ned knew beyond a shadow of a doubt that his sister was in love with the Earl of Cortland.

He looked across at Nathan Walker and said, "Pleased with yourself, aren't you?"

Nathan did not answer as he remounted his steed, turned the horse away and left Egan Grange. His errand had been successfully executed. He wasn't about to bandy words with a child!

Neddy grimaced. "You're a rum'un in my books, Nathan Walker, and this won't fadge, mark me."

Lady Anne lay back against the cushions of her soft blue sofa and sighed heavily. She was heartily bored. The prospect of an evening at Amelia Burney's did nothing to excite her interest. The only reason she was even attending Amelia's rout was because the earl was Arthur Burney's close friend and was therefore sure to be there. Indeed, she needed another chance to work her wiles with the difficult Earl of Cortland. This was due to the fact that things had gone exactly as she had carefully planned. However the earl had not really responded to her advances.

She waved this off. He was no longer a boy, ready to be taken in. But Anne did not welcome challenges. She did not wish to openly chase a man unless he meant to greet her with his arms wide open. There too, she had thought he wanted the tract of land she now owned. She had hoped to dangle it like bait, but he no longer seemed interested in purchasing it. Drat! The price of that piece could have kept her in London for two seasons. Drat, again! Things were not proceeding according to plan. Indeed, things were not running smoothly, but she was not giving up quite yet!

She got to her feet and pulled the rope for her maid. She would choose her most flattering gown, she would dress her golden locks perfectly, and she would make another attempt to dazzle him at the Burneys' that night!

Bess Cornes knocked on Sophy's door and it was an urgent sound. Sophy was seated at her window seat gazing out at nothing in particular. She had gone through a crying bout, then heavily sighed away her tears. This was absurd. One did not go into a decline because a handsome fellow turned your head with a kiss and a smile. This very nearly made her burst into tears again, however, Bessy's insistent knocking made her collect herself enough to call out, "Come in."

Bess opened the door and stood on its threshold, dropping a curtsy to say, "I beg yer pardon, miss, but I've been keeping mum and it ain't right. Johnny, he made me promise him, but I've got to tell ye, warn ye."

"Warn me?" Sophy was surprised into attention. "About what, Bess?"

"The Luddites, miss. Ye see, well, please miss, ye won't bring m'Johnny's name into it?"

"No, of course not. Whatever you have to tell me I will keep in the strictest of confidence," Sophy returned at once.

"Right then, I trust ye, and 'tis with his life, with mine and m'children's lives. Ye see, he works for Branden Mills, he does, and for a pittance. Joined the Luddites in the hopes that if all the men banded together the government might help them, ye see. Well, that's not happening and he thinks he best not attend any more meetings. But there is more. The runner, he isn't jest looking to hang the Luddites. He is looking for *King Ludd*."

"I see, but, why are you telling me this?"

"Because," Bess was wringing her hands. She adored Sophy, but there was no telling how the gentry would behave when you told them something they didn't want to hear. "Well, the thing is, one night when Johnny was cutting through Egan land to get to the meeting, he came across a man in a hood, the hood King Ludd always wears. The man had fallen, gotten his leg caught, and Johnny was helping him up when the hood slipped and he saw in a quick flash who it was. T'was dark, miss, but there was no mistaking who it was." Bess blushed to say, "Miss Sophy, that . . . that man was . . . was . . . your father." Bess looked down at the dark Oriental rug beneath her feet.

"I don't believe it, there must be some mistake?" Sophy

was shocked into responding, but was touched by the truth of what Bess had recounted.

Bess shook her head, "There is no time to be thinking that. I'm telling ye now, cause when I was in town before, I heard that miserable little runner questioning Mr. Grimms. Don't ye see, the runner is bound to be coming here next."

Sophy did see, all too clearly. "Thank you, Bess." She hugged the woman. "You are very good. Thank you." She waited for Bess to drop a curtsy and then, bolstering herself, went out of her room, down the hall, down the stairs and made for her father's study. She was going to get to the bottom of this, once and for all!

Twenty-seven

Sophy went into her father's study and stood, arms akimbo as she tapped her foot and waited for him to look up. He did, and he was taken aback by her expression. "Sophia, whatever is wrong?"

"You tell me, father. Tell me about King Ludd, tell me all about him, because rumor has it that we may be related."

He smiled ruefully. "You have never minced words, have you, dear?" Miles Egan set aside his papers and sighed heavily. "I rather feared that it would come to this when that young man who helped me some nights ago accidentally caught a glimpse of my face. I could see what he thought and I see now what you think. No, Sophia, I am *not* King Ludd."

Sophy's arms dropped as she went forward, and a sob escaped her lips as though it had been wrenched from her heart. Her father immediately got up from his desk and went to her. He put his arms around her and, speaking softly, attempted to assuage her confusion. "I know that is how it looks, but it is not so. I am not so lost to my political beliefs that I would behave in a manner that could be construed as criminal." He shook his head. "I am acquainted with the gentleman who is known to the Luddites as King Ludd. We were literary acquaintances. I don't agree with his need to evoke change even through violence. However, he has on several occasions asked if I would write a speech for him. I thought my peaceful views about how they could work to attain reforms for themselves might be beneficial." He shook his head as he released Sophy to touch her chin. "I did not want them to riot in Nottingham, and believed that I would be able to stave that off here. Thus far, I have been successful."

"Then what were you doing in the forest, with a hood?"

"I was delivering a speech, as I always do, at a designated spot. King Ludd picks up the speech and gives it at the meetings as his own. If they riot, even Cobbett will denounce them. King Ludd knows that and has welcomed my help these past few months. However, 'tis obvious, my love, that I would not wish to be seen."

"Papa, Grimms has told the Bow Street Runner that you have written about treason."

"Grimms is an idiot. My essays are published documents. No one has construed them in that light before."

"Yes, but—"

Stendly knocked at the door, was invited to open it by Sophy's father, and had scarcely enough time to announce Mr. Harold Ingrams and Mr. Oscar Bently before they went barging past him in their rush to get to Sophy.

"Oh, Mr. Egan, you here?" said Harry lamely. He was desperate to speak to Sophy and give her news about the runner's questionable activities.

"Yes, Harold, I am here," smiled Mr. Egan gently. "Well then, why don't we all be seated and then talk, for apparently, it seems that we must."

Harry and Oscar, feeling deuced uncomfortable and very much like wayward children, looked at one another and proceeded to do what they were told.

* * *

Nottingham boasted many refined establishments, but one in particular was an elegant hotel patronized by the Beau Monde. As it happened, it was just as Harry and Oscar sat for a frank talk with Sophy and her father, that a tall, suave, and fashionable gentleman and his entourage entered the charming portals of Nottingham's St. George Hotel.

Upon close inspection, he might even have been considered by some to be quite beautiful, so captivating were his dark, florid looks. His valet hurried about, issuing orders for his lordship's comfort, while his driver took his expensive chocolate colored barouche and matched bays to the livery.

He was taken with great flourish and attention to his suite, and it could be seen that passing chambermaids eyed him with undisguised awe. He was Count Jacques Gérard Laugier and rumor had it that he was one of the wealthiest French emigrés ever to come to England.

Lucinda and the earl were seated for their afternoon tea, though the earl's aunt was still clucking her tongue over the lack of furniture. The earl grinned. "Sorry you came?"

"Ha! A very good thing I did, let me tell you," retorted his aunt severely. "You have made a mull of it with pretty Miss Egan, but never mind. I don't mean to allow you to continue in your folly."

He wagged a finger. "Now Lucy—"

"Don't think you can hoax me, Chase. I haven't attained my numbered year's without learning a thing or two about such matters. I have seen the way you two look at one another."

"She will scarcely look at me at all!" returned her nephew in some agitation. "She thinks I am some old roué, no doubt after her virtue. Who can blame her?" He ran his hand through his wavy hair. "Aunt, she saw that blasted woman kiss me."

"Anne? When? Oh Chase, how could you?" Lucinda returned in some disgust.

"She took me by surprise and then there they were, Nathan and Sophy, across the way."

"Yes, I have no doubt Nathan contrived to have Sophy there, but darling, you gave him the fodder. Took you by surprise, indeed." The earl did not have time to splutter as Hedley appeared at that moment in the dining room's arched entrance. He cleared his throat as he stood portentously waiting to catch the earl's attention. He was quite proud of his morning's work.

"Hedley, come in, and let's have your news," the earl managed to say though his mind was in a frenzy,

"Aye, and news it is I have, m'lord. Things couldn't have moved any sweeter."

"Well, I am glad of it. I wish I could say the same." The earl, like a boy, made a face in his aunt's direction. Lucinda, much in the same fashion, pulled a face back at him. Hedley opened his eyes wide but chose not to comment, waiting patiently as the earl returned his attention to him to ask, "Did you witness his arrival?"

"Aye, had his shot paid in advance, as ye asked, by that friend of mine. There will be no connection to us, as Pat is from Rawlings way and not known hereabout." Hedley grinned in his elfin manner. "Set up a prime story he did, jest as ye wisht."

"Good, good. And what of the runner?"

Hedley scratched his chin. "Well now, m'lord he be a

restless fellow, looking to advance himself at Bow Street. He has certain notions in his head, he does, and it sounded to me like he means to follow through on 'em. But I did manage to get him to promise to pay his respects to ye in the morning. Told him ye were dashed uncomfortable with all of these comings and goings so close to the Abbey."

"What did you think Hedley, does he think he knows who King Ludd might be?"

Hedley shook his head. "Couldn't tell, m'lord. If ever there was a tallow-faced little snirp, that's Mr. Riggs, but I'll say this for him. He knows his job. He says that no one is above the law, and no one is above suspicion." Hedley rubbed his small nose. "The thing is, you be in the right of it cause I got the feeling he be looking in the direction of Egan." Hedley snorted. "There was a moment when I thought he was accusing ye, said something havey cavey was going on near Cortland Abbey and I felt m'fist itching to draw his cork. But he changed his tune and said ye was too new in the neighborhood to know aught of King Ludd, so I let it lie."

"Wise, my man, very wise," grinned the earl. "The thing is, I can not believe Miles Egan is King Ludd, so what then is his part in all this, for a part he certainly has played."

"Ask him," said Lucinda with a shrug of her shoulders. "There is, I am certain, a logical explanation."

The earl grinned as he bowed to his aunt. "Very direct and perhaps, the best approach."

Lucinda smiled superiorly. "Yes, I think so."

Count Laugier entered Amelia Burney's ballroom with something of a flourish and captured a great many glances for he was quite devastatingly handsome. He immediately went to his hostess to bend low over her hand and drawl with his beautiful accent, "Lady Burney, how kind of you to send me an invitation to your rout. *Mon Dieu,* I do not know how I would have passed the evening otherwise?"

Amelia Burney's hazel eyes glittered with amusement. "Why Count, as soon as I heard you had come to town, how could I not?" She turned to her husband and said brightly, "Darling, you remember Count Laugier?"

Her tall husband turned his gaze for the fraction of a moment toward the earl standing some distance away, surveying the new arrival with interest, and he restrained himself from winking in his friend's direction. "Yes, of course we met briefly in London. What brings you to Nottingham, Count?"

"Why, Laugier!" Lady Hester's shrill voice could be heard as she sped across the crowded room hands extended, "Darling, Laugier, here in Nottingham? I had no notion you were coming to us this spring?" She gave him both her hands and winked up at his handsome face.

He held her hands to his lips and whispered, "Lady Hester, *moi,* I am enchanted, this makes for me everything perfect."

Lady Anne had noticed the handsome stranger's entrance and watched with keen interest as Hester went to greet him. She was in a fit of agitation for she had been trying to gain the earl's full attention for the last fifteen minutes, but he would not be caught. Instead, he was following that young redhead about like some lovesick puppy! It was most infuriating and very nearly humiliating as well. She wanted to show the assembled company that she couldn't give a fig for the Earl of Cortland. Anne had just begun looking about for someone interesting enough to flirt with when in walked one of the most handsome men she had ever clapped eyes on in her life. As luck would have it, she was standing close enough to Amelia to lean over and say, "Why, my dear, *who* is this?"

Amelia's brown ringlets bounced as she turned to Lady Anne to say, "Oh, I *am* sorry. I did not see you standing there. Allow me to introduce you. Count Jacques Gérard Laugier . . . Lady Anne Bartholomew." She left them to one another and moved off toward the earl.

"Well, Chase, you are not doing very well, are you?" Amelia nodded in Sophy's direction, for Sophy had virtually snubbed him a moment ago when she walked off on Harry's arm.

He pulled a face and responded, "It is not as bad as it looks. Something tells me the lady cares and I don't mean to give up easily."

"Chase, if you had orchestrated that particular scene yourself, it could not have gone more smoothly." She glanced toward Lady Anne and the count.

"What makes you think I did not orchestrate it?"

She laughed, "Nay, you could not. At least not everything."

"We shall see what we shall see. But what I see now is an opportunity to accost the apple of my eye." He was looking at Sophy, for Harry had just gone off to fetch her a glass of negus, leaving her momentarily unattended.

"I like Sophia Egan so I wish you luck," said Amelia as he started off.

"Thanks as I surely need it." He grinned happily and strode quickly toward his prey.

Sophy felt him coming before she saw his approach and her heart began to beat wildly. Suddenly he was there and leaning toward her ear. "Pretty Red, am I so out of favor?"

Sophy blushed. "What can you mean? Why should you be?"

"I don't know, *you* tell me," he teased and regarded her expectantly.

"I did not say so." Sophy looked around for Harry.

"Harry is delayed, fairly nobbled by some of his friends. Now tell me, is it because I stole a kiss from you? Shall I beg your pardon? I can not. I wanted that kiss and do not regret it."

"Do you always take whatever you want, my lord?"

"No, not if I think it will do someone harm," he answered on a serious note. "I have no wish to do you harm, my love, quite the opposite. Have you not guessed?"

"Guessing is not easy when facts obscure the vision," she quickly looked away from his blue eyes. "Please, I don't mean to keep you from Lady Anne. The two of you must have so very much to catch up with." There she had said it and now felt a complete and utter fool. He must think her a jealous child?

The earl took both her shoulders into his hold and then stopped himself as he glanced round. Without another word he took her hand and pulled her out of the crowded ballroom to the small study across the hall. Sophy made a feeble objection, but thought it best not to create a scene. She found herself suddenly alone with him and being crushed into his strong embrace. His mouth closed on hers, thrilled her beyond reason, and vanquished all logic.

He came away from that kiss to murmur, "You little fool, now what do you think? Tell me."

Think? She couldn't think? She couldn't breathe and she certainly couldn't speak.

"Anne," he said derisively and his lips formed a sneer, "has always been what she is, but I was a boy and didn't see past the pretty face." He shook his head. "Do *you* think I am still that boy?" He shook her shoulders. "Do you?" She tried to answer, but no words came to her rescue. He frowned at her. "Apparently, Miss Egan, you do."

The door opened to admit Harry and Oscar, and Sophy made a desperate rush toward them. She choked back a sob to say, "Harry, Oscar. There you are."

The two lads looked doubtfully toward the earl before following Sophy back across the hall to the ballroom. However, once there, she went directly to her father and, claiming a dreadful headache, asked him to take her home. Some moments later, the earl exchanged a look with Amelia as he watched Sophy take her leave of the Burneys. All at once, he felt empty, and whatever had glittered before seemed to fade. He stood a long moment in a fit of the dismals before a familiar voice at his side ruefully said, "Too much too soon. It is no more than that, nevvy, so don't look so disheartened. The child is in love with you." Lucinda touched his arm reassuringly.

"No, she hates me. Lucy, she fled from here like I was the plague. She knows about Anne and thinks it is Anne I want. She can't know me, as I thought she did, not if she thinks I want Anne."

"What an absurd thing to say," Lucinda scoffed. "Men are such idiots. She is jealous and does not know what to think. If you want her, blow her doubts to smithereens Chase Cortland. Don't play games. Tell her how you feel. If you want her, tell her so."

The Earl of Cortland frowned at his aunt, "But *she* does not want *me.*"

"No? Well, time will tell."

Twenty-eight

The count found Lady Anne extremely desirable and made no secret about it. He was hardly able to leave her side for a moment. Lady Hester smiled to watch the pair and gave the earl, who stood chatting with Amelia and Arthur Burney, a meaningful wink.

Anne was in full bloom. She very nearly blushed beneath the count's avid attentions. She could see from a corner of her eye that the earl was staring at them and she was most certainly gratified to think that the earl was more than a little bit jealous. She proceeded to encourage the count in a most bold and audacious fashion. He touched her arm as they moved and she was struck by a sensation that sent a rush of desire through her. Indeed, here now was a conquest particularly if he was rich.

"La, but Count Laugier, you are trying to turn my head, and will in the end break my poor heart." Anne's lashes brushed her cheek in a most becoming fashion.

"Moi? Never! May I be tortured at the stake before ever I could do such a wicked thing? *Non, mais non.* For you my heart beats tonight."

Lady Anne made a show of sighing. "You can not mean such a thing. We have only just met." She pressed her bare shoulder against his hard lean chest.

He took her hand and put her fingertips to his mouth.

"Moi, I mean the things I say. I am struck tonight," his hand went to his heart, "here and I am undone."

"Ah, you say that now while we are close, while we are touching. The champagne we sip goes to your head, but, alas, tonight will end. Then, you will leave Nottingham soon after and I shall be only a memory."

"No, no, my enchantress. Leave? Now that I have found you? *Mais non!* I shall not leave you." He waved off the objection. "Is it possible you do not know? Did Lady Hester not tell you? *Moi,* I am here at her instigation, *oui,* it is true."

"What do you mean?" Anne looked up at him in some puzzlement.

"Ah, my family, we are, as you must be aware, emigrés. We left Paris and Napoleon a few years ago and came with our fortune to London. My father died last year before we could establish a family seat, so it is up to me to do this. My man of business tells me that land is plentiful here in the north. Lady Hester tells me hunting is especially extraordinary in Nottinghamshire. And *moi,* I have found something else to keep me here."

"You mean you are here to buy an estate, in Nottinghamshire?" Anne's mind began calculating.

"Oui, or build one," said the count glibly. *"Moi,* I make up my mind very quickly about all things." He was staring hard into her lovely eyes.

Lady Anne smiled to herself and said softly. "I am glad. There is nothing more exciting than a man who knows what he wants and sets about to have it." She pursed her cherry lips at him and felt his hand move tightly over hers. Oh yes, she thought as his touch thrilled her, here now was a catch indeed!

* * *

Sophy went to bed and found herself crying in her pillow. She berated herself and forced the memory of every single moment she had spent with the earl that evening to come to life in her mind. He had been so very pointedly attentive, so self-assured, so very gentlemanly. She, on the other hand, had behaved as though her lease of infancy had some years still to go. She had snubbed him and behaved no better than a cockatrice. If only she had it to do over.

After all, he had not spent his time chasing after Lady Anne. No, in fact, he had scarcely looked at the blond beauty. Sophy tossed for a few moments as the meaning of this forced itself on her. Could she have been wrong in assuming he still wanted Lady Anne? It was what Nathan had said. The earl had kissed Lady Anne. Or had she kissed him?

Sophy sat up, punched her pillow a few times and set it in her lap. Well, what did it matter? She had made a roaring fool of herself. She hadn't even been able to answer him. What must he think of her now, after she ran out with Harry and Oscar and left the rout? She certainly knew what she thought of him. She loved him with her entire being and that was a feeling she had never known before. What, just what was she going to do now?

It was a perfect spring morning and Nathan Walker had dressed to the nines. He wore his best coat, cut by Weston himself. It was a pale grey superfine. His waistcoat was an ivory color embroidered with silver. His cravat was tied neatly, if not in the very height of fashion, and his light brown hair was combed in silky waves. This was the morning he meant to propose to Sophia. He had applied to her father late in the afternoon on the previous day, and while Miles Egan seemed a bit taken aback, he said he had no objection to the match, though he had said it was a decision only his daughter could make. Well, it was time she made it.

Nathan had not been invited to the Burneys' affair, but he excused them for this oversight as they were not really well acquainted. He had been only mildly agitated as he really would have liked to have been there to further his courtship of Sophy. However, he was not overly concerned as he had not one doubt in his mind that she would accept his proposal of marriage. After all, she had adored him only two short years ago. Only the earl had come along to take her off course, but he had been successfully routed. Nathan poured himself a snifter of brandy, though he did not ordinarily drink at such an early hour, he felt the occasion warranted it. He raised it and silently toasted himself as he awaited Sophia.

The new morning brought a glorious spring day in full sun. It also brought Sophia a head full of woe. She sighed as she went about getting up, for she had not slept long nor had she slept well. She bathed and quietly allowed Bess to help her dress in a morning gown of soft ivory muslin trimmed with ivory lace. Bess brushed Sophy's long red tresses until they glistened and tied them with an ivory silk ribbon at the top of Sophy's head, where they fell to her shoulders in bouncing ringlets.

Then Sophy received the news that a visitor awaited

her in the library and her green eyes came alive. "A visitor? Who Bess?"

"There, that's better, miss. You do have such a pretty smile. Why, 'tis that nice Mr. Walker come to call."

Sophy's shoulders sagged. "Oh. Yes, of course, please have Stendly serve him coffee and tell him I shall be down in a few minutes." Nathan Walker was one of the last people on Earth she wanted to see.

Oddly enough the earl had slept very well indeed. Well, upon further consideration perhaps it was not so very odd after all. He had reviewed Sophy's words, his own words, and had decided his aunt was in the right of it. Of course, why had he not realized? Absurdly, like a man in love for the first time, he was filled with excitement. His elation did not even subside when he received Mr. Riggs early that morning and discovered that the little fellow actually believed that Miles Egan was King Ludd!

"That, of course, is quite preposterous," the earl answered him immediately.

"Is it, m'lord?" asked Riggs sweeping his moustache with thumb and forefinger. "Well now, Oi 'ave reason to believe otherwise."

"What, from a disgruntled employee? Nonsense. Miles Egan would have had to be something of a magician if he were King Ludd."

" 'Ow is that?"

"King Ludd by all accounts was in the heart of Manchester inciting to riot, while Miles Egan was here in Nottinghamshire, attending to his estates, which is a fact that can be easily corroborated by his family, his servants, and the local people. Facts are facts. In the meantime, I feel I must tell you that I have every intention of writing your superiors and advising them of your irresponsible behavior in this matter. A man's reputation is at stake, Mr. Riggs, and you can not be allowed to tarnish it without just cause."

Mr. Riggs fidgeted. "Well now . . . Oi ain't accusing nobody, am Oi?"

"Are you not? I am glad of it. Then allow me to advise you that Nottingham is a peaceful town and whatever meetings these poor weavers have held have not been to incite riot. However, there is a different climate in the north, near Manchester, where I am told only some days ago Luddites were smashing machinery and destroying private property. If you mean to advance yourself, you might wish to make the journey there to conduct your investigations?"

Mr. Riggs knew his business. He did not really believe that Miles Egan was King Ludd, instead he suspected that Miles Egan knew King Ludd and hoped to use Egan to flush out the fellow. However, there was some truth to the earl's calculated words. "Aye, might do that when Oi check out the dates of the last riot in Manchester and the alibi you say Egan has."

"Allow me to caution you, sir. Ask your questions if you must, but make them questions *not* accusations. We understand one another, do we not?"

Riggs understood him very well. He wanted no enemies amongst the nobility. No sense ruffling feathers to no purpose. "Aye, we understand one another. I mean to check some back issues of the *Chronicle* and see when those Manchester riots took place for Oi already know when Egan was about and wasn't about." On this cryptic remark, Mr. Riggs took his leave.

* * *

Anne wore a clinging negligee of soft pink silk and an untied matching wrapper. Her blond curls hung loosely round her lovely face as she opened her bedroom door and allowed Count Laugier to enter.

The count was only a little surprised. In London, ladies of rank often received gallants in a state of dishabille in their boudoirs. However, this was not London, and he had only just met the lady. He knew well how to use the moment and moved quickly as he closed the door behind himself and swept her into his embrace. *"Cherie,* last night I could not sleep and when at last I did it was to dream of you, of this."* He kissed her earlobes, softly wandered down her neck which she gently arched for him. He then followed the line back up to her chin, and his mouth closed deftly over hers.

When he allowed her to breathe, she softly said his name, "Ah, Jacques, it was the same for me. But you must not . . . lest we forget ourselves." She wanted only to give him a taste and thus, tempt him further. She was too well versed in the game. If he wanted more, he was going to have to put a wedding ring on her eager finger! After all, he was no child. She guessed that he was very nearly her own age, perhaps a year or two younger.

"Oui, oui it is not the time. I am a cad. Forgive me," he uttered as he released her and ran his free hand through his black waves of hair. He stood back from her. "I came to ask you to come with me. There is an old estate, it is for sale at a most ridiculously high price, but," he shrugged, "people will put such value on sentiment. At any rate, Lady Hester's man, Harcot, has made arrangements for me to have a look at it, and I would like for you to accompany me, *oui?"*

"Oh my, you do move quickly, don't you?" smiled Anne

much like a satisfied cat. "Hmmm. Yes, I would love to accompany you. Go, darling, down to the morning room and make yourself comfortable while I change." She wrapped her delicate arms around his neck, and kissed him lightly on his lips. "I won't be long."

"Good, it is good that we go together," he said, bowing low as he took a step backward and blew a kiss from the palm of his hand to her.

The earl watched Mr. Riggs leave and found his butler standing in the doorway. "What is it, Woodly?"

"Master Egan, m'lord. He has been waiting . . ." There was no need to say more as Ned charged past the harassed butler to enter the room, go directly to the earl and tug at his sleeve,

"Please, my lord. I need to talk privately with you."

The earl could see that Ned was looking extremely troubled and nodded a dismissal to his man as he said, "Of course, lad. What is it?"

"That was the runner. I . . . I didn't mean to eavesdrop, but I heard him as he was leaving. He thinks m'father—"

"No, he does not, not any longer. I believe Mr. Riggs will be leaving Nottingham very shortly. Rest easy, lad, your father has nought to fear from him."

Ned breathed a sigh of relief and looked at the earl with pure worship in his eyes. "It is you we have to thank for that. I'm sure you managed him, just as you do everything."

"Nonsense. Your father's good name and the facts managed Mr. Riggs. All I did was to point him in the right direction."

"Well, I know the truth of it, but there is more. It is Sophy—"

The earl came to attention. "What? What is wrong with Sophy?"

"Ah, you *do* care. Thought so," said Ned on a pugnacious note.

The earl bent and took Ned's shoulders. "What is toward, Ned? *Now,* if you please!"

"Well, it is Walker. By now I suppose he has already proposed to Soph, and I don't want him for m'brother-in-law." He shook his head dejectedly. "Didn't think Soph wanted him either, but she knew why he came, father told her and she wouldn't let me say she was too sick to receive him."

The earl stiffened. "Are you telling me that you think Sophy means to accept his suit?" Jealousy raged through him, hurt slapped away all earlier logic.

"The thing is girls sometimes act queer, don't you think? And Soph might be piqued because Nathan told her you and Anne were going to make a match of it. I know cause I heard him just yesterday."

"Ah, so I have Nathan to thank for that, do I? Well, I suppose he felt all was fair in love." The earl's eyes glinted with sudden anger.

"I don't know about that. I only know that you have to do something," said Ned taking a halting step toward the door, *"Now!"*

"Thank you, Ned."

"Well, is that all? Aren't you coming?"

"For now, I think not," the earl answered quietly.

"Don't you mean to stop her?" Ned demanded in disbelief.

"If Nathan Walker is the man she wants to marry, so

be it. She is old enough, wise enough, to know her own mind." Jealousy was pinching his heart, freezing his mind.

Ned shook his head. "I thought you liked Soph."

"There is more to it than that."

"No there isn't," spat Ned in disgust. "Grownups always make things more complicated than they have to be." So saying he turned on his heel and left the earl to himself.

Chase Cortland looked up at the clock on the fireplace mantle. It was too late. If Nathan Walker had proposed by now Sophy had given her answer, and if she had accepted him, then that was that!

Twenty-nine

"No, no, this is not the one. The house is in ruins, it has a bad odor. It is not worthy of my family name. No, I can not bring here my bride," the count looked meaningful at Lady Anne, "which is what I desire." He sighed sadly and sat back against the luxurious squabs of his plush barouche. *"Moi,* I am surprised Lady Hester's man sent us to such a place?"

A bride? Anne's eyes clicked into focus. "Perhaps it could be renovated?" She knew there were very few estates for sale in the immediate area.

"Oui, this is possible. *Mais non,* it was too dark. *Moi,* I must have something grand with windows and doors to the garden. Ma petite, did you like this puny place?"

Anne shook her head. In truth she did not think it so very bad, however she did not wish to contradict him. Rather she worked her wiles and agreed with all his decisions, but she did want him to purchase something immediately and secure him in Nottinghamshire.

"No, but 'tis not," her voice dropped to a demure octave, "for me to say . . ."

"You mistake. *Moi,* I do not like that old dark house, *mais* if you, *ma belle,* did I would purchase it for your pleasure." He took her hands and kissed them passionately.

"Jacques," she whispered and then sighed. "Oh dear, but I am certain you will find something else."

"No, I must build! *Oui,* this I would like. Would you like this, *cherie?*"

"Yes, yes I would." She could picture a house being built to suit her every whim. Indeed, that was exactly what she wanted!

"Alas, I must find a suitable tract of land. We will go to Lady Hester and ask her to find us some."

Anne's eyes lit up. "No, we will not! Darling," she became very animated, "as it happens I have a large, empty beautiful plot that is not attached to Bartholomew land. A lovely stream winds through it, it is perfect for what you want! In fact, Harcot knows of it and I am surprised he did not mention it to you. No doubt Cortland instructed him to keep quiet about it." There, she thought. Chase Cortland, you shall lose your land forever! What a perfect revenge for his rejection.

"Mais oui, you must show this land to me at once!" He held her for a long moment. *"Cherie,"* he whispered as he kissed her, "Fate has brought us together."

Sophy knew why Nathan had come, but she was the sort that faced and dealt with distasteful matters as quickly as she could. She managed a smile as she entered the library to greet Nathan. He came forward and lifted both her hands to his lips. She hurriedly withdrew them and put up a hand as though to ward him off.

"Nathan, we are friends. So, I must tell you—"

"Friendship makes it all the sweeter, does it not?"

"No, it does not. It makes it deuced difficult." Sophy tried to smile but could not. "I am your friend and that is why I don't want you to ask . . . what you came here to ask."

"Sophia." Nathan frowned his objection. "Perhaps, you don't really understand why I am here."

"Oh, but I do." Sophy took a step away. "Nathan, we are so very different from one another. I am fairly certain I should drive you mad with my antics. You must see we simply would not suit. Please forgive me, but plain speaking is something I do. I am not the sort of woman you need."

"Sophia, you are the only woman I need." He followed her to take her shoulders in his hold. "Your father does not object, I spoke with him yesterday."

"I know. Don't you see, we are worlds apart. You do all that is proper. I don't give a fig for propriety. If my father had objected, would you still have come to me?"

"This is absurd. He did not object." Nathan was losing patience.

"If he had, would you still want me?" Sophy pursued to make her point.

"Of course, I would want you, but I would not be in a position to offer for you, at least until I was able to convince your father otherwise." Nathan's lips were set in a hard line. This was not progressing the way he had imagined.

"There, you see. I want someone who would offer for me regardless. You will say that is romantical nonsense, but that is what I need." She shook her head. "My father did not object, but I am afraid I must." She smiled softly. "We were meant to be friends, Nathan, nothing more. You must not be sad, I am doing you a favor."

Nathan Walker pulled himself up to his full height and raised a cold brow. "Obviously. I now see that you are. Good day to you, Sophia. I shall not be calling again, as friend, or otherwise." So stating he promptly picked up his hat and left the room.

Sophy sank into a nearby chair and dropped her head into her hands. "At this rate, Sophy, you shall be an old maid. You don't want Nathan, or anyone other than the earl, and the earl apparently does not want you." This notion sent a wave of self-pity through her that set her to weeping once more.

The earl was on tenterhooks waiting for Nathan Walker to return to the Abbey. He left a message at the stables for Nathan to attend him as soon as he arrived, but noon came and his architect was still not about. It was then that Woodly appeared with a sealed letter from Walker.

The earl took it to his desk and was about to break the seal when his aunt burst into the room. "Chase! I have just come from Hester's," she saw his expression and immediately asked, "What is it? What is wrong? What have you there?"

"Nought," he replied, putting the unopened envelope down. "What has Hester to say?"

"It is what her spies have to say," Lucinda laughed merrily. "All is progressing very swiftly."

"Good," he answered but he was still frowning.

"Good? What do you mean, good? You have gone to a great deal of trouble and expense and all you can say to the success of your well laid out plans is, good?" She shook her head. "Now, that is quite enough. Whatever is wrong, Chase Cortland?"

"Nathan Walker has proposed to Sophy," the earl responded in bleak tones.

"Is that all? So?" returned Lucinda laconically.

"Lucy, if she has accepted him nothing will have any meaning for me. All will be lost." He hung his head. Until this moment he had not really understood how very much he loved Sophia Egan. It was she that held the key to all his needs. The thought of losing her was almost more than he could bear.

"Sophia Egan does not want Nathan Walker and if she *has* accepted him, the fault will lie at your door," returned his aunt in caustic tones.

He ran his hands through his hair. "What shall I do?"

"Well, how do you know that Nathan has proposed? Where is he? What makes you think she has accepted?"

"Walker told her of my history with Anne. He led her to believe that Anne and I are lovers. Sophy thinks I played her false when I stole a kiss from her."

"You stole a kiss from her?" Lucinda's brows were up. "Well then, 'tis time you stole another." She shook her head. "If you show her how you feel, Chase—"

He cut her off. "It is no doubt too late." The earl took up the letter and stared at it. "This is from Walker—"

"Open it!" demanded his aunt on a note of exasperation. "Really, men can be so very stupid!"

He managed a half smile but did as he was told and read out loud,

My lord,
    Some personal business takes me away for a few days. When I return, I will have the sketches prepared for the East Wing.
        Yours respectfully,
        Nathan Walker

"Well, that doesn't sound like a man who has just become engaged, does it?" Lucinda said thoughtfully.

"Yes, it does. Very much so. A man who is about to get married would have personal matters to attend to, would he not? There is the license and any number of things he might have to arrange for their wedding." The earl wandered restlessly around the room.

"Then, my buck, you are out of time!" snapped his aunt, "Up, get up and go to her at once, if you want her, and tell her. At this point you have nothing to lose."

"Unless I have already lost her."

Lucinda shook her head. "In all other matters you would take up arms and fight for what you want. You have displayed just how fierce you can be with the business of Anne and the land she meant to withhold from you! Will you fight any less fiercely for the woman you want? You have a great deal more at stake now, Chase. What are you going to do about it?"

He eyed his aunt for a long moment and suddenly a glint came into his blue eyes as he said, "I suppose if I must go down, I shall go down fighting." So saying he took her shoulders in his strong clasp and dropped a kiss on her forehead before he stormed out of the room shouting for his horse.

Sophy sat on a stone bench in the rose garden and to all outward appearances she seemed intent on watching the roses bloom. She pulled the shawl the earl had given her tightly around her shoulders and sniffed away a tear.

The earl saw her from the drive even before he had dismounted his steed and given the reins over to an approaching groom. He looked at her in her ivory lace and muslin, with her red ringlets all about her beautiful face. There was no other woman for him, only Sophy. What would he do if she had already accepted Nathan Walker? He strode quickly across the lawn to where she sat.

Sophy was so lost to her misery that she never heard his approach. All at once it seemed he was there, taking her hands into his strong hold, pulling her up from the bench and wordlessly, breathlessly enveloping her in his embrace. His kiss was desperate as his mouth closed on hers and cried for her response. Sophy clung to him as though he were a miracle. When he allowed her to breathe it was to fervently tell her, "You will be *my* wife not Nathan's, not anyone else's. Sophy, I love you. No other man can make you happy. Do you hear me Sophy?"

She nodded that she had, and was once again crushed in his arms. After a moment, she managed to push a little bit away and look up at him to inquire, "Did . . . did you apply to my father first?"

He looked thunderstruck. "No, oh forgive me, Sophy. Should I have? I suppose I should."

She laughed wildly and flung her arms around him. "No, oh, Chase no."

As she put her hand up to stroke his face, he whispered softly, "Sophy, I love you," and this time his kiss was touched with the tenderness he felt throughout his body. "I have so much to tell you, to explain to you—"

"Later," Sophy responded, as she reached up to kiss his lips. "Much later."

However, this kiss was rudely, but happily, interrupted by Ned, who came upon them to declare, "Yes, by Jove, yes. She says yes!"

Epilogue

A week later the earl was driving his betrothed to town, and they stopped along the road to watch a young lamb playing near its mother. He drew Sophy into his arms and sighed contentedly. They had announced their engagement in the *Nottingham Chronicle* and had set their wedding date for early June. Nathan had returned and had taken the news in stride, though he had not yet encountered Sophia. Harry and Oscar eyed one another with rueful grins and agreed that Sophy's husband would have his hands full, whereupon, they immediately allowed another local beauty to catch their fickle affections.

Sophy giggled as she watched the lamb play and then stroked the earl's cheek to ask, "What I don't understand is how you managed to arrange for the count to make an appearance so quickly?"

"The count and I met on the ship when I was returning from India. We became fast friends. However, he has no fortune as it was lost to Napoleon when his family fled to Italy." The earl grinned. "He decided to make his living at something he does well . . . gaming. I decided to make an investment and we went into a partnership of sorts in a club, a very exclusive gaming club the count runs successfully in Derby, which is not so very far from us. I sent for him, and as I said, since we are friends he came at once. As it happens, he is very successful with the ladies."

"Hmmm, I have no doubt of that," said Sophy and her green eyes glittered appreciatively.

"You like his good looks?" the earl inquired casually.

"He is very, very handsome. I can see why Lady Anne was charmed so readily."

"I see." The earl stiffened.

Sophy giggled and pinched his cheek. "However, he is far too pretty. *I* prefer your very rugged good looks."

The earl took her into his arms and held her tight. "I should hope so."

"Yes, but fortunately Lady Anne was charmed by him. Did he actually propose to her and then leave? I don't think that is right."

"He did not. She led him on, he led her on. He paid her an outrageous price for my land and then transferred it to me when I advanced him the money to close the deal. It was all very legal."

"Where does she think he has gone?"

"He left her saying he had family matters in Italy to attend to. After a time, she will learn that the land is mine, and I will say simply that I purchased it from the count, who decided against building here in Nottinghamshire. As I said, it is all very legal." His blue eyes glittered.

"And devious," Sophy said softly, "as you were with my father, I am sure. How else did you get him to send Neddy to Harrow?"

"With logic," was all the earl would say.

"Logic? I have tried to use logic and it never worked."

"Timing is everything." So saying he bent to kiss her lips.

"Aha!" said Harry riding up behind them with Oscar.

"There you are. Don't forget we are due at Wendells for the cockfight this afternoon." Harry and Oscar had amiably decided that the earl was a right 'un they would include in their lively set.

When Oscar noticed that the earl and Sophy had been kissing he blushingly nudged Harry along, tipping his hat and saying that they were expected at their friend's house and were already late.

Sophy watched them ride off and turned to giggle, "As you were saying, something about *timing,* my lord?"

He answered her with a kiss, long and sweet!

ZEBRA REGENCIES
ARE
THE TALK OF THE TON!

A REFORMED RAKE   (4499, $3.99)
by Jeanne Savery

After governess Harriet Cole helped her young charge flee to France—and the designs of a despicable suitor, more trouble soon arrived in the person of a London rake. Sir Frederick Carrington insisted on providing safe escort back to England. Harriet deemed Carrington more dangerous than any band of brigands, but secretly relished matching wits with him. But after being taken in his arms for a tender kiss, she found herself wondering— *could* a lady find love with an irresistible rogue?

A SCANDALOUS PROPOSAL   (4504, $4.99)
by Teresa DesJardien

After only two weeks into the London season, Lady Pamela Premington has already received her first offer of marriage. If only it hadn't come from the *ton's* most notorious rake, Lord Marchmont. Pamela had already set her sights on the distinguished Lieutenant Penford, who had the heroism and honor that made him the ideal match. Now she had to keep from falling under the spell of the seductive Lord so she could pursue the man more worthy of her love. Or was he?

A LADY'S CHAMPION   (4535, $3.99)
by Janice Bennett

Miss Daphne, art mistress of the Selwood Academy for Young Ladies, greeted the notion of ghosts haunting the academy with skepticism. However, to avoid rumors frightening off students, she found herself turning to Mr. Adrian Carstairs, sent by her uncle to be her "protector" against the "ghosts." Although, Daphne would accept no interference in her life, she *would* accept aid in exposing any spectral spirits. What she never expected was for Adrian to expose the secret wishes of her hidden heart . . .

CHARITY'S GAMBIT   (4537, $3.99)
by Marcy Stewart

Charity Abercrombie reluctantly embarks on a London season in hopes of making a suitable match. However she cannot forget the mysterious Dominic Castille—and the kiss they shared—when he fell from a tree as she strolled through the woods. Charity does not know that the dark and dashing captain harbors a dangerous secret that will ensnare them both in its web—leaving Charity to risk certain ruin and losing the man she so passionately loves . . .

Available wherever paperbacks are sold, or order direct from the Publisher. Send cover price plus 50¢ per copy for mailing and handling to Penguin USA, P.O. Box 999, c/o Dept. 17109, Bergenfield, NJ 07621. Residents of New York and Tennessee must include sales tax. DO NOT SEND CASH.